PRAISE FOR

# I KILL THE MOCKINGBIRD

"*I Kill the Mockingbird* is a novel that speaks of mighty things
in the midst of an ordinary summer—well, in the midst of a
hysterically funny ordinary summer. Its adventure has one goal:
to extol the glory of reading. But Acampora, the sly dog,
has something else to extol, too: the glory of living."

## —Gary D. Schmidt,

Newbery Honor–winning author of *Okay for Now*

"Smart, funny, and touching, usually in the same sentence!
A true book lover's book about how one story
can make a huge difference."

## —Wendy Mass,

author of *Jeremy Fink and the Meaning of Life*

"Paul Acampora's unique gift is that he sees the absolute best
in people. When you see his lovable characters in action,
you will, too!"

## —Jordan Sonnenblick,

author of *Drums, Girls & Dangerous Pie*

"Fans of the Harper Lee classic—and book nerds everywhere—should flock to this uplifting, unabashed tribute."
—**The Horn Book**

"The banter among the three whip-smart friends would make John Green proud. . . . You won't have to hide any copies of this to create demand."
—**The Bulletin**

"Acampora's well-written, resolutely cheerful offering celebrates books, reading, and life."
—**Booklist**

"Funny, poignant, and quirky."
—**School Library Journal**

"Fans of Janet Tashjian's the Gospel According to Larry series will enjoy this look at how the power of creativity and the Internet can cause a cultural movement. . . . Acampora's novel is for lovers of literature, especially how the classics work in the current moment."
—**VOYA**

"Literary terrorists hit Connecticut, but things go awry for a trio of well-meaning book addicts. . . . The spot-on dialogue combines with the irresistible appeal of young teenagers enthusiastically pursuing bad ideas for a fast, page-flipping read."
—**Kirkus Reviews**

"This strong novel stands on its own as a testament to the power of reverse psychology, but will resonate with fans of the original *Mockingbird* and maybe inspire a few to check it out."
—**Publishers Weekly**

# I KILL THE MOCKINGBIRD

## PAUL ACAMPORA

SQUARE
FISH

ROARING BROOK PRESS
NEW YORK

SQUARE
FISH

An Imprint of Macmillan
175 Fifth Avenue
New York, NY 10010
mackids.com

Square Fish and the Square Fish logo are trademarks of Macmillan and
are used by Roaring Brook Press under license from Macmillan.

Square Fish books may be purchased for business or promotional use. For information on bulk
purchases, please contact the Macmillan Corporate and Premium Sales Department at
(800) 221-7945 x5442 or by e-mail at specialmarkets@macmillan.com.

Library of Congress Cataloging-in-Publication Data

Acampora, Paul.
    I kill the mockingbird / Paul Acampora.
        pages cm
    Summary: "When best friends Lucy, Elena, and Michael receive their summer
reading list, they are excited to see To Kill A Mockingbird included. But not
everyone in their class shares the same enthusiasm. So they hatch a plot to get the
entire town talking about the well-known Harper Lee classic"—Provided by
publisher.
    ISBN 978-1-250-06808-8 (paperback) / ISBN: 978-1-62672-057-2 (e-book)
    1. Lee, Harper. To kill a mockingbird—Juvenile fiction.  [1. Lee, Harper. To
kill a mockingbird—Fiction.   2. Books and reading—Fiction.   3. Friendship—
Fiction.]  I. Title.
    PZ7.A17298Iak 2014
    [Fic]—dc23

2013044998

Originally published in the United States by Roaring Brook Press
First Square Fish Edition: 2015
Book designed by Elizabeth H. Clark
Square Fish logo designed by Filomena Tuosto

10  9  8  7

AR: 4.1

For Mom & Dad

# CONTENTS

· · · · · · · · · · · · · · · · · · ·

· · · · · · · · · · · · · · · · · · ·

# 1
# The Queen of England Is in Our Bathroom

. . . . . . . . . . . . . . .

*My mother's wheelchair does not fit through the bathroom* door, and I don't know what to do about it. I pull the chair back an inch and then roll it into the door frame again. The *clunk* makes Mom sit up straight. "You have got to be kidding me," she says.

Actually, these are not her exact words. I am not allowed to repeat her exact words.

"Don't worry," says Dad, who stands inside the bathroom, ready to give Mom a hand. "We'll figure something out."

This is the first time my mother has been home from the West Glover Hospital in over a month. They only let her leave because she promised to stay off her feet for at least forty-eight hours. I put my hand on Mom's shoulder. "What if we turn it around and back it in?"

"Lucy," Mom says to me, "width is not a function of vector."

Mom studied math in college. She's a professional photographer now, but she's always finding ways to work things like vectors and differentials and Hilbert curves into conversation. I rarely know what she's talking about.

"We don't have vectors in our math," Elena calls from the kitchen.

"We'll get to them in high school," says Michael, who is in the kitchen, too.

Michael Buskirk and Elena Vallejo are my best friends. They were both on the front lawn waiting to greet Mom when we got back from the hospital. The three of us met back in kindergarten when Elena was a black-haired bulldozer in a pink dress and a leg brace, and Michael was a quiet skinny boy in short pants and Space Invader T-shirts. Now we are all in the eighth grade at St. Brigid's Catholic School, where my dad is our principal.

Elena sighs. "Vectors and high school," she says. "I can't wait."

Elena is certain that high school is going to swallow us up, spit us out, and crush us like bugs. It's because she still looks like a little doll that Santa Claus would leave beneath a Christmas tree. I resemble one of those gawky stuffed giraffes that nobody ever wins at the carnival, but Michael is over six feet tall. He's strong and easygoing with dark hair and brown eyes that match the color of his skin. I think he's the best-looking boy in our school. He lives just across the street from me, so I see him enough to know that I'm right.

"Elena," Dad shouts from the bathroom. "Please stop worrying about high school. It's months away, and it's going to be fine."

"How do you know?" she yells back at him.

"It's one of the things they teach you in principal school," he tells her.

"He's got you there," Michael says to Elena.

"In the meantime," says Mom, "I still really have to pee." A few wisps of thin, brown hair have escaped the paisley scarf wrapped around her head. Dark circles beneath her eyes make it look like she's been punched in the face. Cancer will do that to you.

Dad examines the doorway leading into the bathroom. "We'll get another inch of clearance if I take the door off the frame." At school, I've seen him unclog toilets, mop up vomit, set a broken bone, and rescue a wide variety of rodents, snakes, amphibians, and other classroom pets without even loosening his tie. Popping a door off its hinges is not going to be a problem.

Michael hops off the kitchen counter. "I'll get the toolbox."

"There's a screwdriver in the junk drawer," says Elena.

The two of them know where everything is. They've pretty much grown up in our house, and sometimes we're more like family than friends. I love having Elena as a sister, but lately I'm thinking it might be nice if Michael were a little less brotherly and a little more friendly. That's another door I don't know how to get through.

"How about we just do this?" says Mom. Without waiting for an answer, she places both hands on the wheelchair's armrests and pushes herself into a standing position.

"Whoa!" I say.

Dad quickly reaches an arm around Mom's waist then takes her hand. "May I have this dance?" he asks.

Mom takes a breath. "Lead me to the toilet first."

My parents say it's the everyday moments—folding laundry, washing dishes, pouring each other a cup of coffee—that make their marriage a good one. I know they're right, but I'm hoping for something a little more romantic than a stroll into the bathroom one day.

With Dad's help, Mom takes a small step forward. "Are you okay?" I ask her.

Mom takes another step then places a free hand on the sand dollars and sea fans and junonias that decorate our bathroom wallpaper. "I'm happy to be home."

"And cancer free," says Dad.

She nods. "That too."

A year ago, the doctors explained that Mom's disease—something with a name that sounded like *angie-mumbo-jumbo-plastic-lycanthrope*—was rare, aggressive, and generally fatal. In other words, she had a roughly zero chance to live. Even *I* understood that math. A week ago, those same doctors announced that she was cured. "How is that possible?" I asked.

The doctors shrugged. Sometimes, they told Dad and me, it just happens. Afterward, one of Mom's nurses found us in the hospital corridor. "God heard your prayers," she said. "That's how it happened."

It's true that we'd been doing a lot of praying, but until now it didn't seem like anybody was really listening. "I don't know about that," I said.

"God heard you," the nurse said again. "It's a miracle." And then she burst into tears.

Neither Dad nor I backed away. I think it's because we

both spend our days in Catholic school. That's where you learn that faithful people can be a little insane sometimes. On the other hand, is it more sensible to accept that everything is random or is it better to believe that God can step in occasionally and repair your T cells? I don't know.

Either way, Mom is on her feet now. She's moving forward with Dad on her arm as if they are about to meet the Queen of England in our bathroom. Mom even offers dainty royal wrist waves as she exits the hallway. This should be funny, but I don't laugh. I suppose this is the result of even more Catholic school stuff filling up my head. We're taught that sometimes the world is a puzzle waiting for us to solve it. Other times it's a mystery to appreciate and accept. Right now I think my family, my friends—maybe even my whole life—are a whole lot of both.

# 2
# What Would Fat Bob Do?

. . . . . . . . . . . . . .

*After a few days, Mom can use the bathroom by herself.* After a few weeks, it's clear that she really is getting better. Before I know it, the last day of eighth grade has arrived. Miss Caridas, who is our English teacher today and will be our English teacher again next year at St. Patrick's High School, scratches a list of book titles onto the board. "These are your summer reading choices," she announces.

Miss Caridas recites each title aloud as she writes it down so that the list is revealed in a weird kind of slow motion.

"*David Copperfield*

"*Ender's Game*

"*Fahrenheit 451*

"*War Horse*

"*War of the Worlds*

"*The Giver.*"

And finally,

"*To . . .*

"*Kill . . .*

*"a . . .*

*"Mock . . .*

*"-ing . . .*

The class sighs.

*"-bird."*

I've already read most of these books. Michael has, too. Elena's probably read all of them twice. Her Uncle Mort runs a used bookstore in the center of town, and we've been helping out—and sometimes just hanging out—in the shop for as long as I can remember.

Elena lives with Mort in an apartment above the bookstore because her parents died in a big car crash when she was just a baby. Elena was in the car crash, too. Obviously she survived, but that's why she used to have the leg brace. Except for a very slight limp, which you wouldn't notice if you weren't looking for it, that part of Elena's life is ancient history. According to her, it's a book that nobody wants to read and she doesn't want to open. "But don't you miss having parents?" I asked Elena once.

She just shrugged. "I have Mort," she told me. Mort was her mom's big brother. "He gives me food. He gives me shelter. He gives me love. He gives me all the free books I can read. What part of the parenting thing am I missing?"

Miss Caridas finishes writing. She replaces the marker on the ledge and claps her hands together. "Any questions?"

I have a question: Why do teachers think that shoving summer reading lists down our throats is a good idea?

I turn to St. Brigid whose picture hangs on our classroom wall. She's our school's namesake as well as the patron saint of dairymaids, chicken farmers, and children whose parents are not married. I don't fit into any of St. Brigid's categories, but I mutter a little prayer to her anyway. "Please," I say, "can this school year be over now?"

St. Brigid says nothing. Of course nobody else is speaking, either. Around me, my classmates hardly move. I'm not sure that any of them are even awake.

"People!" our teacher shouts. "*Atención!*"

Miss Caridas grew up in Puerto Rico, and she pulls out the Spanish whenever she really wants to get our attention. She's been with us for most of the year, but I still think of her as a substitute. Dad hired her after our first teacher, Mr. Robert "Fat Bob" Nowak, died in the line of duty.

Mr. Nowak was as big around as a Volkswagen. He started every day by printing W.W.F.B.D? (WHAT WOULD FAT BOB DO?) in giant letters across the top of the whiteboard. He died in the St. Brigid cafeteria just before Halloween. I was standing beside him on the day it happened. He was paying for his lunch, and the cafeteria lady at the cash register asked, "Do you want fries with that?"

"Fries would be—" Mr. Nowak stopped. He stepped back. He put a hand on his chest. "Good." He took a breath. "Fine." He looked around the cafeteria. "Wonderful."

He sounded almost wistful, which is when I knew something was wrong because St. Brigid's fries are good, but they do not inspire wist.

"Mr. Nowak?" I asked. "Are you okay?"

His face was bright red. His breathing sounded suddenly difficult. For some reason, he turned toward a shelf filled with a whole bunch of pre-wrapped sandwiches. Most of them were egg salad. "Lucy," he said, "I've been teaching for a lot of years, and let me tell you something." He tried to take a deep breath. "You've got to enjoy every sandwich."

"Mr. Nowak," I said, "I don't like eggs."

I wish I had responded with something a little more meaningful, but at least it made him laugh. He leaned against the cafeteria wall. "Don't be afraid, Lucy."

I still didn't understand what was happening. "Afraid of what?"

"Anything. Everything. Be brave." He took a cell phone out of his pocket. "And now I'm going to call 911."

I felt my pulse began to race. "What are you talking about?"

He stared at his phone and then laughed again. "This is going to sound crazy, but I think I forgot the number for 911."

"It's nine—"

Before I finished speaking, a massive heart attack dropped him to the floor. He went down like a boxer on the wrong end of a knock-out punch. "Help!" I shouted. From there, I remember ambulances and stretchers and sirens in our school. None of it mattered. Fat Bob was dead.

Miss Caridas arrived not long after that. She is young and pretty. She graduated from college at the end of last May. Sometimes she doesn't seem much older than us, but she is much stricter than Mr. Nowak ever was. I think she thinks that she has to be. Now she takes a neon-orange yardstick from the ledge and taps it against the board. "You will choose at least four titles from your summer reading list to enjoy once at your leisure, and then you will review them again before ninth grade begins. Each work contains its own symbolic vocabulary that . . . blah, blah, blah . . ."

I stare at the space above Miss Caridas's head that used to say W.W.F.B.D?

WHAT WOULD FAT BOB DO?

Mr. Nowak definitely would *not* have served up a long list of summer reading options. "*To Kill a Mockingbird* is the only book I will assign over your next summer vacation," he told us back in September. "By then you'll be good enough readers to appreciate it."

I remember thinking, *I'm already a good reader.*

"You might be thinking that you're already a good reader," Mr. Nowak said.

More than a couple of us shifted in our seats.

"It's not enough to know what all the words mean," he continued. "A good reader starts to see what an entire book is trying to say. And then a good reader will have something to say in return. If you're reading well," he told us, "you're having a conversation."

I raised my hand. "A conversation with who?"

"With the characters in the book," said Mr. Nowak. "With the author. With friends and fellow readers. A book connects you to the universe like a cell phone connects you to the Internet." He tapped on the side of his head. "But it only works if your battery's not dead."

That made us laugh. Mr. Nowak liked to make us laugh. He told us stories about his life before he became a teacher. He actually had a short career in the Canadian Football League. After that, he had some success as a professional wrestler. "In the high stakes world of professional wrestling,"

Mr. Nowak told us, "Fat Bob was six feet eleven inches tall. He weighed four thousand pounds. He was feared on seven continents, and he was a three-time International Smackdown Champion of the Universe. Several nations classified Fat Bob's left hand as a lethal weapon."

"Is any of that true?" we asked him.

"Every word," he promised.

"You don't really weigh four thousand pounds," we told him.

"Catholic school does not require my full fighting weight," he explained.

"You're not six feet eleven inches tall."

He shrugged. "Old age makes you shrink."

When he died he still needed a casket that was as long as a minivan and as big across as two double-wide refrigerators. On the day of the funeral, the huge box rested on a set of broad blue straps stretched across an aluminum frame over an open grave. Father Wrigley, our pastor at St. Brigid's, led us through final prayers. A dark-suited funeral director approached the coffin and stepped on a small lever in the grass. Slowly, Mr. Nowak lowered into the ground. As the box descended, Father Wrigley said, "This day is not just an ending. It is—"

The priest was interrupted by a loud SPROING!

Then there was a SNAP! And a PING! And a WHIRRRRR!

The straps supporting the coffin started to unwind like a fishing line hooked into Moby Dick. Fat Bob, who'd been going down about an inch a minute, accelerated into the pit with all the force that gravity can muster on an almost four-thousand-pound man. In case you're wondering, that's a lot of force.

"Sweet Jesus," said the funeral director.

The casket roared into the ground like a fighter plane crashing out of the sky. The box disappeared from view, but the straps buzzed and whined until a muffled *BOOM!* brought everything to a halt. There was a cloud of dust. I was dimly aware of shouts and chaos. A woman standing near Father Wrigley stumbled back in a faint.

Our whole class moved forward to stare into the grave. Shiny pieces of metallic blue casket lay scattered below. All four sides of the coffin had burst apart. It looked as if a Lincoln Continental had exploded down there.

"Oh my," said Father Wrigley.

Dad stood as open-mouthed and shocked as the rest of us. Standing in a cemetery beneath a bright blue autumn sky was the last thing my father or I wanted to be doing that day. Nobody but Michael and Elena knew, but my mother had just entered the hospital to start getting filled with cancer drugs and radiation treatments.

*Timing,* Mom says when she's shooting wedding photos, *is everything.* Standing over Mr. Nowak's open grave, it struck me that the rule might also apply to funerals. I wouldn't be surprised if it comes up in other situations too.

"Mr. Jordan?" one of the Clooney twins said to my dad. "What should we do?"

My father looked down at our big dead teacher. Dad studied the bent and broken casket. Finally, he turned to the Clooney boy. "What Would Fat Bob Do?"

It wasn't really a question. It was more like a challenge or even a dare. And I knew exactly how to respond.

*Don't be afraid! Be brave! Enjoy every sandwich!*

But I could not speak. I stared into the grave and said nothing.

Now, the last bell of the school year interrupts my thoughts. Suddenly, my classmates are wide awake. In fact, we are all on our feet and moving toward the door. "Have fun this summer!" Miss Caridas calls after us. "Be safe! Don't forget to read!"

There's excitement and yelling and laughter as we exit the classroom. There is also some mumbling and complaints.

"Do you think she gave us enough to read?"

"Are there movie versions of these books?"

"School is over. I'm not doing homework."

I'm swept up in a crowd of kids heading toward the doors. "Mr. Nowak said that *To Kill a Mockingbird* was pretty good," I remind my classmates.

"I'm spending my summer at the beach," a boy replies. "If you want to spend it at the library, go ahead."

I stop walking and the crowd flows past. "You know what," I say. "Maybe I will."

# 3
# Hippopotomonstroses-quippedaliophobia

. . . . . . . . . . . . . . .

*On the first day of summer vacation, my mother stands* with her hands on her hips staring across our backyard at Elena and me. "Honey," Mom calls to Elena, "the Virgin Mary's head should not look like a portobello mushroom."

Elena grins. "Sorry, Mrs. Jordan."

Mom crosses the yard, grabs the blue bedsheet wrapped around Elena's head, and gives the fabric a tug. Somehow the adjustment makes my friend look a lot more biblical. "Much better," Mom says, then returns to her camera.

Every year, right after school lets out, Mom sets up a life-size birth-of-Jesus scene beneath the pine trees in our backyard. She uses it to create photos that she'll sell for church calendars and Christmas cards. Last year, Michael, Elena, and I posed as shepherds. The year before that we were the Three Wise Men. This year it's just Elena and me. I'm dressed as Joseph, and Elena is pretending to be Mary.

"Lucy," Mom asks me, "why does Joseph look like somebody just died?"

Beneath my Joseph costume—a tattered wool blanket, a gray thrift-store wig, and a fake beard taped to my face—I am a sweaty mess. "Joseph is about to pass out."

Mom stares at me through her camera lens. "You can blame Michael for that."

Michael is supposed to be the one wearing the Joseph get-up, but he's playing baseball today. In fact, he's supposed to have two games this morning. Dad says that Michael is good enough to play in college. Maybe he'll even be in the pros one day. I just wish he was here with us now. It's tradition. On the other hand, Mom would have kept Elena in the Mary outfit, Michael would have played Joseph, and I would have had to pose as a camel or a cow or something equally attractive. "Were there giraffes in Bethlehem?" I wonder out loud.

"I've been thinking about that, too," says Elena.

"You have?"

She rolls her eyes. "No. But there is something I've been meaning to ask you."

"What is it?"

"Michael likes you."

I feel as if the star of Bethlehem has just fallen out of the tree branch above us and knocked me in the head. "You know," I say, "a question is supposed to have a question mark in it."

"I think you like him, too."

"We're friends."

"You know what I mean."

I glance down at Elena. "Do you even know what a question is?"

15

Mom leans away from her camera. "Tilt your heads up," she tells us. "And pull your shoulders back." She glances at a few bright rays of sunlight beaming through the trees. "Those are going to give me some angle of incidence issues," she mutters.

"You're speaking math again," I call out, but she ignores me. Her arms still look like twigs, and her skin is the color of vanilla ice cream. I don't think she should be out in the sun yet, but it's not like I can tell her what to do.

"So?" says Elena.

"So what?"

"So what are you going to do?"

I take a deep breath to try to slow down my pulse rate. "I'm going to try to avoid having heatstroke."

"I'm talking about Michael."

I lift the hem of my shawl and wipe it across my face. "I'm not."

Elena swivels her hips, reaches between her legs, and adjusts her costume. "If it makes you feel any better, this Virgin thing isn't too comfortable either."

"What's going on?" Mom calls from the other side of the yard.

I rub a drop of sweat off my nose. "The Blessed Virgin has her shorts in a twist."

"I need the two of you to stand still."

Elena and I get back into our Joseph and Mary poses. "But seriously," she whispers to me. "What are you going to do?"

"Why do I have to do anything?"

"You don't."

"That's right."

16

"But you should."

"Like what?"

Elena throws her hands up. "I'm the Virgin Mary! How am I supposed to know?"

"Now what?" shouts Mom.

"Nothing!" says Elena.

"Sorry!" I say.

"Can we get serious?" asks Mom.

"Okay." Elena sticks a somber drama club expression on her face. "I am serious."

"You look terrified," I mutter.

She nods toward a plastic baby doll that Mom's placed on a bale of hay. "I am portraying a teenage girl with a baby here. Terrified is the appropriate emotion."

"I need you to look like you're filled with wonder," Mom calls to us.

Elena considers the instruction then turns to inspect the plywood shed and the stuffed farm animals propped around us. "If I am the Mother of God, then I *wonder* why I just gave birth in a barn." She turns to me. "Joe, you couldn't do a little better with the accommodations?"

"You fell for the first angel that came along," I say. "This is what you get."

Elena gazes up at the sky and sighs. "He looked like Johnny Depp, and he promised he'd show me heaven."

A loud laugh interrupts us. It's my father standing on the back porch.

"Hey, Mr. Jordan!" calls Elena.

Dad waves. He has a coffee cup in one hand and a newspaper in the other. Despite his black-rimmed glasses and the flecks of gray hair, Dad carries himself like the all-star athlete he used to be. He can still grab a glove, a stick, or a racquet and give just about anybody in West Glover a run for the money. Dad glances at Mom and gives her a quick once-over. "How are you feeling?" he asks her.

Mom stands up straight. She runs a hand through her hair. "Fine."

Mom's regained a lot of strength, but she's not back to her old self yet. I want so badly for her to be well. Also, a guarantee that there will be no cancer in her future would be nice. Actually, I want to turn back time and stop her from getting sick at all. Since that's not possible, maybe I could grab a gigantic megaphone and shout at God, the world, and everybody, "HOW DID YOU LET THIS HAPPEN?"

"Girls," Dad calls to us, "can we get this done?"

Elena pumps her hand in the air and shouts as if she is running for president. "Yes, we can!"

Mom rubs her chin and smiles a little. "Elena," she says, "it's a good thing you're cute."

The Virgin Mary squeals. "I'm cuuuuuuuuute!"

Mom leans back toward the camera. I adjust my blanket. Elena fixes her sheet. From there, we settle down and do our best to look serious or wonderstruck or whatever. It must be working because Mom gets all the photos she needs in less than fifteen minutes.

"Stick a fork in us," Mom says. "We're done."

"Amen," I say.

"Merrrrrrrry Christmas!" Elena shouts.

"Thanks, girls," Mom says.

Dad helps pack up the camera equipment and move it

back into the house. I begin gathering plush sheep and cows and donkeys. "Lots of girls would like to go out with Michael," Elena tells me.

I stuff a load of felt snouts and furry tails into a plastic storage bin. "That's nice."

"But not you?"

I don't answer.

"Why not?"

The pine branches above us, which are usually filled with birds and squirrels chirping and chattering, grow suddenly quiet as if even the wildlife wants to see what I have to say. "Michael is my friend. I don't want to mess that up."

Elena nods thoughtfully. "You're afraid."

"I'm not afraid of anything."

"Everybody's afraid of something. Personally, I struggle with *hippopotomonstrosesquippedaliophobia.*"

"Very funny."

*Hippopotomonstrosesquippedaliophobia* is a word that Mr. Nowak used to put on our spelling tests. It means the fear of long words.

Elena puts her hands on her hips. "If you're not going to do anything, then I'm going to tell Michael that I have a crush on him."

I stop in my tracks. "You do?"

Elena laughs. "Not really. I just wanted to see your reaction."

"That wasn't funny." I turn and consider my friend. "But why don't you? I mean we've all been together forever. You know Michael as well as I do. Why do I feel this way and you don't?"

19

Elena shrugs. "This might sound silly, but when I have a boyfriend, I hope I can kiss him without using a step stool."

"That makes sense," I admit.

"It makes sense now," says Elena. "But one day I'll probably get swept off my feet by the Jolly Green Giant."

"Or somebody like Fat Bob," I say.

"I'm going to set the bar a little lower," Elena tells me. "Literally. But you don't have to."

I think about what Elena is saying. "Okay," I finally reply. "I'll talk to Michael."

Elena retrieves a pink pig from the grass. "That's good."

I remember another one of the big words that Mr. Nowak taught us how to spell. "But I'll do it chronogrammatically."

Elena looks perplexed. "You're going to speak in Roman numerals?"

Now it's my turn to be confused. "I thought that chronogrammatically meant saying things in your own time."

"Chronograms are words or phrases that have letters like M or C or L or V. The letters tell a date written in Roman numerals."

"Why exactly do you know that?" I ask her.

"I live in a bookstore," she reminds me. Elena gathers the Virgin Mary sheet around her shoulders. "Saying what you mean is hard enough, Lucy. Then you go and add seven or twelve or fourteen extra syllables for no good reason. Pretty soon, we're back to the Tower of Babel." She shakes her head. "It's a little scary."

"Elena," I say, "you're a little scary."

"That's why you love me," she says, "but don't call me little."

# 4
# Jesus in a Bike Basket

. . . . . . . . . . . . . .

**Once Elena and I finish gathering the stuffed animals,**
we drag the rest of the manger scene into the garage. We
have a two-car garage, but my parents rarely squeeze more
than one vehicle in here. Dad's Jeep lives in the driveway,
and Mom's Volkswagen, which hasn't left the garage in
months, stays inside. Right now, the VW is surrounded by
several old bikes, a rickety wooden stepladder, and a big red
snowblower.

Elena places our plastic baby Jesus inside a wicker basket that's attached to the handlebars of an adult-sized tricycle near the Volkswagen's back bumper. Somebody donated
the three-wheeler to St. Brigid's, so Dad brought it home in
case Mom wants to use it while she's recuperating. St. Brigid
herself will come back from the dead on a skateboard before
my mother chooses to pedal around West Glover on a tricycle.

"Want to go for a ride?" Elena asks me.

I shove the last box of Christmas decorations into a corner. "Sure," I tell her.

"Can I ride the tricycle?"

I point to a big wire cargo bin that's fastened behind the trike's seat. "We'll have to put something heavy in there or else it tips over really easily."

Elena moves the plastic doll from the basket to the bin.

"Baby Jesus is not enough," I warn her. "You've got to have a lower center of gravity." I find a small, unopened bag of rock salt and place it into the bin next to the doll. "Now you should be okay." I grab the pink princess three-speed that my parents got me when I turned ten. It's too small for me now, but I still like it. "We're going to the Green," I shout into the kitchen.

"Okay," Dad calls back.

"Michael is playing baseball at the Green," says Elena.

"So?"

She shrugs. "I'm just saying."

Together, we pedal away from the garage and then down the driveway. I'm behind Elena, and I see one wheel of the tricycle lift slightly off the road when we turn onto the road. "Be careful!" I call after her.

"Don't worry!" She stands on the pedals and speeds away.

We roll down my street, and Elena waves at my neighbors. Michael's driveway is empty, which means that his mom is probably cruising around town in a West Glover police car. During the school year, she's the police officer who makes classroom visits encouraging kids to read books, stay off drugs, pick up trash, learn how to swim, put out forest fires, and grow up to be president one day. When she's not at work, Mrs. Buskirk is a coach for a bunch of different youth softball and baseball teams. As for Michael's dad, neither Elena nor I have ever met him. Michael gets Christmas and birthday cards from his father now and then, but he's not part of the family photo album.

Elena and I stop at the signal light on Main Street. If we turn right, we'll reach Uncle Mort's bookshop. If we turn left, we'll see the West Glover Public Library, which is just a block away. Instead, we cross Main Street then keep going straight. One more block brings us to the Federal Green, a wide, open park at the heart of our town.

Back in Puritan days, West Glover's Federal Green held a community sheep grazing pasture, an outdoor market, and a set of stocks and pillories for troublemakers to endure public humiliation. Now it's home to tall gnarled sycamores, a brightly colored play structure, and a couple rough, mowed baseball fields. There's a soccer field and a big, white bandstand, too.

The metallic clank of an aluminum bat echoes across the park. Elena and I turn toward the baseball diamond and pedal through the grass. The baby Jesus bounces around the tricycle's storage basket like a kangaroo on a trampoline until we finally stop at the wooden stands near the first-base line. That's where we find Michael, all dressed up in his green-and-white Little League uniform. He's sitting by himself in the bleacher's first row.

Elena cruises to a stop beside the bleachers. "What are you doing?" she says to Michael.

Michael looks up from a worn copy of *Fahrenheit 451*. "What does it look like I'm doing?"

"It doesn't look like baseball."

"I played in the first game. They asked me to sit this one out."

"Why?" I ask him.

"I hit four home runs."

Elena remains in her tricycle seat. "So?"

"And seven RBIs."

"Seven is a lot," I say.

"It might have been eight." Michael scuffs his shoes in the dirt. "And then they kicked me off the team."

"Excuse me?" asks Elena.

Michael shrugs. "After my last home run, the coach on the other team complained. He says I can't be fourteen years old."

"But Michael," I say, "you are fourteen years old."

Michael nods toward the opposing team's bench. "According to them, I'm sixteen or eighteen or thirty-seven."

Elena stands on the tricycle's pedals. "That must have been some home run."

Michael points across the Green at the big white-steepled church in the distance. "It landed on the steps of First Congregational."

Elena stares at the church, which is across the street from the Green. It's more than a football field away. "That's a big league home run!"

"Look where it got me," Michael tells her.

"That's not fair," I say to Michael.

"You've got to call your mom," Elena adds.

Michael points to the opposite side of the Green where a

couple tiny T-ball teams are running around. "She's over there helping the little kids."

"Do you want me to get her?" I ask.

"No." Michael reaches into an old *Star Wars* backpack that's sitting by his feet. He finds a water bottle, takes a long drink, and then sets the container on the bench. "The other coach was right."

Elena hops off the tricycle. "You're thirty-seven?"

Michael shakes his head. "I should be playing against tougher competition."

Just then, a batter sends a pop fly into shallow left field. The shortstop, the third baseman, and an outfielder all rush to make the catch. They collide and then collapse onto the ground.

"You might be right," I tell him.

"I'm waiting for this game to finish," Michael continues, "then I'm going to ask the coach if he'll help me sign up for one of the senior leagues. That way, I can go up against high school and college players this summer. It's the only way I'm going to get better."

"Fine then," Elena says. She points toward Michael's backpack. "What else did you bring to read?"

"You don't have to sit around too," Michael tells her.

"We'll wait." She leans back and gives me a wink.

I try to give her a mean face, but it's no use. Elena does what she wants. I don't know how she manages it. In so many ways, she's had no control over her life. She lost both her parents. Her body got all wrecked and then reassembled by strangers and she was passed off to an uncle who, luckily, is really nice. Her life has been a roll of the dice. And yet she is so strong and funny and sure about things.

"It's up to you," Michael says. He places his copy of *Fahrenheit 451* on the bleachers then reaches into the *Star Wars* backpack and pulls out two more paperbacks. "Do you want *David Copperfield* or *To Kill a Mockingbird?*"

Elena takes *Fahrenheit 451*. Michael turns to me. I don't speak. I just hold out my hand. Michael smiles. "One *Mockingbird* coming up."

# 5
# A Mob. A Horde.
# A Multitude. A Throng.

. . . . . . . . . . . . . . .

**Here's the thing.** To Kill a Mockingbird *is my favorite* novel of all time. When Mr. Nowak announced that it was his only choice for summer reading, I wanted to jump up and cheer. There are long sections of the book that I know completely by heart. Last year, Michael and Elena even helped me read the whole thing out loud to my mom when she was too sick to do anything but lie down. We sat beside her bed and took turns. Once, when Elena was reading, Mom lay so still that we thought she might be dead. None of us knew what to do. Elena was reading the scene where Atticus Finch, the main character's father, has to shoot a dog that's got rabies. It is a very tense moment, and when Atticus finally pulled the trigger, I burst into tears. Mom opened her eyes. "What's wrong?" Her voice was thick and groggy.

"Nothing," I lied.

"Why are you crying?"

"The book," I said. "The dog—"

Elena shifted in her chair near the foot of Mom's bed. "Mrs. Jordan," she said, "we were afraid that maybe you were—"

"What?" said Mom.

"A little dead," admitted Elena.

Mom took a sip of water. "Don't buy a box for me yet."

My face burned red. Mom wasn't going to get a box. Dad already let me know that he and Mom wanted to be cremated one day. "You can spread us around the graveyard at St. Brigid's," he told me. "We'll be good for the grass, and it will be nice to be near the church."

Mom was in the hospital the day Dad shared that bit of news with me. It was cold outside, and Dad and I were carrying groceries from the car into the house. "Haven't you had enough church?" I blurted out.

"I have absolutely no idea," he told me. "That's why I keep going."

"Why else?" I asked him.

Dad put the groceries on our kitchen table. "Life is a gift. Going to church is like sending a thank-you card."

At our house, thank-you cards are a big deal.

"Mom's cancer isn't a gift."

Dad started putting food away. "Remember when you chipped your tooth last year?"

Without thinking, I ran my tongue over my front teeth. One of them is mostly plastic now. I cracked it during a soccer game in the middle of seventh grade. The boys called me snaggletooth for a week, and I cried myself to sleep every night. "I remember."

"Did you know that I went to high school with your dentist?"

"Dr. Sullivan?"

Dad nodded. "Mary Sullivan was my date to the junior prom."

"I didn't know that," I admitted.

He passed me a bag of fresh broccoli, which I carried to the refrigerator. "I wore a powder-blue, polyester tuxedo with lapels the size of the Bermuda Triangle," Dad recalled. "There was also a matching ruffled shirt and a bow tie that looked like I stole it off Ronald McDonald."

I turned around just in time to catch the red pepper Dad threw my way. "I don't think Ronald McDonald wears a bow tie."

"Now you know why. In any case, Mary and I are still friends. That's why I told her I was worried that your mother had been losing weight. She's the one who called Mom and convinced her to make an appointment with the doctor who found the cancer. I wouldn't have seen Dr. Sullivan if you hadn't broken the tooth."

"So?"

"So did you think that your chipped tooth was a gift from God?"

"No."

Dad waved a roll of paper towels at me. "And yet—"

"There's a big difference between cancer and a chipped tooth."

"I'm not saying that cancer is a gift. Neither is a chipped tooth. But you don't know what will come of it. Personally,

I don't believe that God has motives that we are supposed to understand or enjoy."

"But you still say thank you."

"Good manners never hurt anybody."

A sudden, strong breeze cuts across Federal Green and knocks the cap off Michael's head. He grabs for the hat and drops *David Copperfield* into the grass. Elena takes the book, opens to the beginning, and reads aloud: "Whether I shall turn out to be the hero of my own life, or whether that station will be held by anybody else, these pages must show."

Michael returns the baseball cap to his head. "Charles Dickens is awesome."

"Are you kidding?" Elena holds up *David Copperfield*. "This book is like a sleeping pill."

Michael's mouth drops open. "What are you talking about? Dickens novels are like roller coasters. You have to enjoy the ride."

Roller coaster rides make me want to vomit, but I don't mention that.

"Plus," says Michael, "he puts the whole story right there in the first sentence. That's real writing."

"You want real writing?" says Elena. "You want a first sentence? '*Where's papa going with that ax?*' That's *Charlotte's Web*. That's real writing."

Michael shakes his head. "You are not seriously comparing *Charlotte's Web* to *David Copperfield*."

"I can't," Elena tells him. "*Charlotte's Web* is a good book."

"You are insane," says Michael.

Elena sticks her nose in the air. "My lack of sanity has no

bearing on the fact that you don't know what you're talking about."

Even in kindergarten, Michael, Elena, and I obsessed about books. Not only that, the three of us believed that characters like Winnie the Pooh and Ramona Quimby and Despereaux Tilling actually existed. We fully expected to meet all our favorite characters in person one day. Books carried us away. They'd definitely carried me through this past year.

Michael takes *David Copperfield* out of Elena's hands. "Just so you know, Charles Dickens was more popular than *The Wizard of Oz* and *Harry Potter* combined."

I glance over the top of *To Kill a Mockingbird*. "I don't know about that."

"It's true," says Michael. "Dickens's novels came out in monthly installments. People couldn't wait for the next chapters to arrive. Mobs would gather at train stations and shipyards so they could be first in line to get the next part of the book."

"Mobs?" I say.

"Hordes. Multitudes. Throngs."

"I know what a mob is."

"People don't feel that way about books anymore," Elena says sadly.

"Some people do," I say.

"Not around here," she replies.

"Elena," I say, "we live around here."

"Lucy," she tells me, "we're weird."

Just then, we hear the umpire's call from behind home

plate. "*STRIKE!*" A smattering of applause and cheers makes it clear that the game is over.

Michael stands. "I don't mind being weird."

He jogs toward the dugout where one of the coaches greets him kindly. I see the man nodding and patting Michael on the back. It looks like things are going to work out baseball-wise. In the meantime, Elena climbs back aboard the tricycle. "You know," she says, "we should start a mob."

"A what?"

"A horde. A multitude. A throng."

I glance up at the blue sky above us. On the horizon, a few puffy clouds look like they might be carrying rain, but right now it's a perfect summer day. "I know what a mob is. What are we going to do with one?"

"We will speak for the books."

"Like the Lorax?" When we were little, *The Lorax* was our favorite Dr. Seuss book.

"Exactly."

"The Lorax speaks for the trees," I remind her.

"Books are made out of paper. Paper is made out of trees."

"What about e-books?"

"We can speak for them, too."

"Audiobooks?"

"Audiobooks speak for themselves." She grins. "Get it?"

Michael returns to the bleachers. "It's settled. I'm moving up."

"Do you want to be in our mob?" Elena asks him.

"When did we get a mob?" he says.

"We don't have one yet. I'm working on it."

Michael turns to me.

"It's got something to do with books."

"In that case," says Michael, "I'm in."

"You don't even know what it is," I tell him.

He shrugs. "My mom says that ignorance rarely stops anybody from doing anything. I guess she's right."

# 6

# Jesus, Ginger Ale, Norse Gods, and Wiener Dogs

. . . . . . . . . . . . . . .

*It's late in the morning, and I can't remember what day* of the week it is. That's one of the things I love about summer vacation: it doesn't matter what day of the week it is. I do know it's a weekday, because Dad is at school. He's at St. Brigid's Monday through Friday doing principal stuff all summer long. Meanwhile, Mom's asleep in a chaise lounge on the back porch. She looks quiet and comfortable. Dad will be home for lunch soon, so I let her sleep and head for Mort's bookshop.

When I arrive, Mort is speaking with Officer Buskirk on the sidewalk in front of the store. "Morning, Lucy," says Mort. "How is your mother?"

"Lots better," I report.

Mrs. Buskirk puts her hand on my shoulder. "That's good news. You give a shout if you need anything."

"Thanks," I tell her. "We will."

Inside, Elena is sitting behind the cash register. She's got her head buried in a novel while Michael steps out of the storeroom with two big cardboard boxes in his arms. Mort, who follows me into the shop, points Michael toward the counter near the cash register. "Right there will be good."

Michael squeezes around tables and chairs covered with magazines and books. He finally makes it to the front of the store and drops the boxes onto a chest-high shelf.

"Lucy," says Mort, "you're just in time."

With his gray beard and gray hair pulled back into a long ponytail, Mort looks like an aging rock star. According to my parents, he's raised Elena as half princess and half business partner. In other words, she can do pretty much anything she wants as long as she helps out at the store and treats the king kindly. From what I've seen, both the king (a.k.a. Mort) and the princess have a pretty good deal.

"In time for what?" I ask.

"The big reveal." Mort pulls a Cub Scout knife from his front pocket and slices open a box.

Elena lowers the paperback she's reading. It's a novel called *Franny and Zooey*. I've read it before, but I don't remember it that well. I point at the book. "Isn't that the one about the girl who lies around the house crying all the time?"

Elena nods. "She stops eventually."

"She stops when Jesus shows up," says Michael.

Elena shakes her head. "Jesus doesn't show up."

"He does too."

"Does not."

"Jesus comes into the kitchen and asks for a glass of ginger ale," Michael reminds her.

"It's only a small glass," I recall.

"I don't even like ginger ale," says Elena.

Michael shakes his head. "You're missing the point."

"If Jesus comes over," says Mort, "you can ask him to turn your ginger ale into grape soda." He reaches into the cardboard box and pulls out several books. They are all brand new copies of *To Kill a Mockingbird*.

"That's on our summer reading list," I say.

"I know." Mort opens the remaining boxes. "I've also got *Ender's Game*, *David Copperfield*, *Fahrenheit 451*, and all the others, too." He stacks the books neatly on the counter. "I've been thinking about doing some kind of online thing to let kids know they can get their summer reading books here. Do any of you know how to do that?" Mort is not much of a computer guy.

"Maybe we could get everybody's e-mail addresses from school?" Michael suggests.

"I don't think my dad gives that stuff out," I tell him.

Elena tosses *Franny and Zooey* onto a nearby shelf. "Nobody reads e-mail," she says. "We need to get everybody's cell numbers and text them." She walks around to the front of the counter. "Or maybe we could use Twitter and Facebook and Tumblr and all that."

"What are you talking about?" Mort says to her.

Before Elena can answer, the front door swings open and a small, dark-haired girl steps into the shop. She's wearing a too-big baseball cap stuffed over a mess of wild, dark curls. A sky-blue T-shirt reaches down to her knees, and she's got a tiny dachshund stuffed into the crook of one arm. The dog has a red, white, and blue collar attached to a long, green leash that's dragging on the ground behind them. "My name is Ginny," the girl says in a very loud voice. "Do you have any dog books?"

Her dachshund squirms and wiggles and wags his tail like a wind-up toy plugged into a nuclear power plant.

"Sure," says Elena.

Ginny examines Elena. The two of them are nearly the same height. "Do you work here?"

"I live here."

Ginny, who can't be more than eight or nine years old, turns around in a circle to take in the entire store. When she's done, she puts her free hand on her hip as if she owns the place. She returns her gaze to Elena. "So do you have dog books or not?"

Elena narrows her eyes. "I just said we did."

"What kind of dog books?" I ask. "Books with stories about dogs? Books about raising puppies? Books about dog training?"

"My dog is very well trained." Ginny places her dachshund onto the floor. Unfortunately, nobody seems to have let the dog know that he's well-trained. The moment his feet hit the ground, he sprints full speed toward the back of the shop. The dachshund's tiny toenails sound like toothpicks spilling across a table top. His leash skitters behind him like a skinny snake trying to catch its supper.

"Hey!" yells Elena.

"Balder!" hollers Ginny.

"Balder?" says Michael.

Ginny glares at him. "That's his name."

Mort laughs.

"What's so funny?" she asks.

"Balder is the Norse god of beauty, light, and joy," says Mort.

"So?"

"So that's a wiener dog."

Just then, Balder's leash snags beneath a knee-high pile of self-help books. Balder gives a loud *YIP!* and a tug. The books topple over, and the dog is off to the races again.

"Could somebody please stop him?" Mort asks calmly.

"Balder!" Ginny shouts again. The dog glances back over his shoulder, offers another excited *YIP!* and keeps going. The dachshund skids around another bookshelf, knocks over a pile of old LIFE magazines, and then stops to chase his tail for a moment. He is obviously having the time of his life.

"I've got him! I've got him!" Ginny moves toward Balder, but before she gets too close the dog sprints away.

"Run, run, run," says Mort, "as fast as you can. You can't catch Balder, he's—"

"—a small Norse god trapped in the body of a wiener dog," I say.

Mort laughs. "That's exactly what I was going to say."

The dachshund appears at the end of a row of murder mysteries. At the other end of the row, Elena squats down so that she is at eye level with the little canine. "Balder!" she yells. "Stay!"

The dog skids to a full stop.

"Come!" says Elena.

Balder stares at Elena's face for a moment as if he's considering the request.

"You heard me," Elena tells the dog.

Suddenly, Balder puts his head down and races toward

Elena at top speed. At the last moment, he leaps into her arms and proceeds to cover her face in licks and kisses.

"Nice job, Frigga," Mort tells Elena.

"Who's Frigga?"

Ginny sits on the floor next to Elena and begins to pet her dog. "Frigga is Balder's mom. She was a queen. She could see the future, but she wouldn't tell anybody about it."

"How do you know that?" asks Elena.

"I read books," Ginny says as if this should be obvious.

Mort reaches down and takes the dachshund from Elena's arms. "I will hold on to Balder," he says to Ginny. "Our friendly staff will help you find some dog books."

"Thank you," Ginny says politely. "I'd like that."

Michael, Elena, and I spend the next half hour assembling a stack of titles featuring great canines. We find used copies of *The Wonderful Wizard of Oz*, *Lassie Come Home*, *The Phantom Tollbooth*, *Because of Winn Dixie*, *The View from Saturday*, and *Babe the Gallant Pig*.

Ginny examines the pile. "Are you sure these are dog books?"

Mort points to a picture book called *Noodle*. Its cover features a simple, bright painting of a sleeping dachshund. "This is a macaroni cookbook."

"I don't believe you," says the girl.

Mort shrugs. "Suit yourself."

Ginny digs a handful of paper money plus a bunch of coins from her pocket. She holds it out toward Mort. "This is all I've got."

Mort takes a five dollar bill and two quarters from Ginny's palm. "You drive a hard bargain."

Ginny puts her change away and retrieves Balder from Mort's arms. "Thank you," she says.

"Come back soon," says Michael.

"And your little dog, too," adds Mort. Once the door swings shut, he sighs. "I love my job."

"You just love chasing wiener dogs," says Elena.

Mort's mustache perks up. "Isn't that what I just said?"

Elena takes one of the *To Kill a Mockingbird* copies that are still stacked on the counter. "We forgot to give Ginny one of these."

"That's not a dog book," says Michael.

"There's a dog in it," says Elena.

"A dead dog with rabies doesn't count."

Elena shrugs. "A sale is a sale."

"That little girl does not want a copy of *To Kill a Mockingbird*," Mort tells us.

"She doesn't know what she wants," says Elena. "That's why she needs us."

"Yes," says Mort, "but we must use our power for good."

"What power?" I ask.

Mort takes out his Cub Scout knife and begins to cut the empty cardboard boxes into pieces that will fit into the recycling bin beneath the counter. "It's the books that have power," he says, "but a good bookstore will influence what a person chooses to read."

I think for a moment. "Does it have to be a good bookstore?" I ask.

Mort considers the question. "Probably not," he finally admits.

# 7

# Holden Caulfield Is Undead and Other Things We Learn at the Mall

. . . . . . . . . . . . . . .

*The next day, Elena, Michael, and I take the bus from* West Glover to the River Road Mall. Inside, the mall's main thoroughfare is all tile and glass and neon storefronts. It makes me think of a carnival midway that's way too clean. Michael stops in front of a fat, fake palm tree that reaches toward the skylights in the mall roof. "Why did we come here?" he asks.

"Because we can," says Elena.

Mort, Mrs. Buskirk, and my parents agreed that the three of us could do a lot more on our own this summer as long as we generally stick together and that we use our cell phones to check in.

We pass a few clusters of teenagers and several bored looking security guards. We weave around two old women in matching blue sweat suits, dodge a remote control helicopter and a robot dog at Ye Olde Toy Shoppe, then stop at the long, blue fountain where a little blond girl in pink shorts, a pink T-shirt, and pink flip-flops is leaning over the water. She's got a coin clutched in her fist, and she's holding it above a little sprinkler that's spraying her hand. She's almost ready to toss the coin into the water and make her wish. Unfortunately, a lady pushing an empty stroller accidentally jostles the girl's elbow. The coin slips from her hand and drops into the fountain with a disappointing *plop*.

"Sorry, honey," says the lady. And then she just keeps going.

"Hey!" I shout, but the woman doesn't hear or else she just ignores me. I turn to my friends. "Did you see that?"

Michael digs into his pocket and comes out with one penny and a nickel.

Elena shows me an empty hand. "I don't have any change."

I take the coins from Michael and approach the fountain where the girl's got an arm stuck in the water up to her elbow. An older woman holds the girl's shoulder to keep the child from falling all the way in. "Grandma!" the girl shouts, "I can't reach!"

"Excuse me," I say.

Grandma yanks the child away from the fountain and turns toward me. "Yes?"

"My wish!" says the girl.

"This is for you." I stuff the coins into the child's palm.

"Oh," the old lady says. "Thank you. Thank you very much." She nods at the girl. "What do you say?"

The child looks down at her hand. "This is six cents."

"You can have it," I tell her.

She looks up at me. "But I had a quarter." Her cheeks get red, and her eyes begin to fill with tears.

"I'm sorry," I say. "That's all I've got."

"You can't make a twenty-five cent wish with a nickel and a penny."

"But—" I stop. What am I going to say? The kid is right. "I'm sorry," I say again.

The girl throws herself into her grandmother's arms and begins to sob. Slowly, I back away and rejoin Michael and Elena. "That didn't go well."

"You offered her six cents for a quarter's worth of wishes." Elena shakes her head. "That's not a fair trade."

"I know," I say, "but—"

"But sometimes life isn't fair," says Elena.

"That's not what I was going to say."

"But it's true. It's like what happened to your mom or to my parents."

I glance back toward the little girl who is still crying near the fountain with her grandmother. "Losing a quarter is not like cancer and car crashes," I say.

"Or how about Fat Bob?" Elena continues. "That was totally unfair."

"Elena," says Michael, "Mr. Nowak didn't die because life is unfair. He died because he had clogged arteries from being three hundred pounds overweight."

"Death by French fries," says Elena. "You don't think that's unfair?"

"I think that's unhealthy," says Michael.

The three of us begin walking away from the fountain. "You know what's really unfair?" I say to my friends. "We

43

hardly ever even talk about Mr. Nowak anymore. It's like he disappeared off the face of the earth."

"Lucy," says Michael, "he sort of did disappear off the face of the earth."

I give Michael a dirty look. "I know he's dead, but it doesn't seem right that we basically forgot all about him."

"That is unfair," says Elena. "Fat Bob was awesome."

"He really was a good teacher," Michael agrees.

"We should do something so people will remember him," I say.

"Like what?" asks Elena.

I shrug. "I don't know. Maybe we'll come up with something while we're here."

Michael glances around. We're surrounded by pretzel shops and shoe stores. "At the mall?"

"You can learn a lot at the mall," Elena tells him.

We turn and wander into a giant bookstore. Inside, we find several large tables holding dozens of different titles on display. There are best sellers, true crime, and tons of discount books. There's also a huge range of recommended and required summer reading from all the local schools. Our St. Brigid titles are mixed in with a predictable set of classics, but there are some unexpected choices, too. I pick up a vampire fantasy that's stacked next to *The Catcher in the Rye*. "Holden Caulfield is undead," I say. "Who knew?"

"Like I said," Elena tells me, "you can learn a lot at the mall."

"How does Mort compete with this?" Michael wonders out loud. The mall bookstore has got to be a hundred times bigger than Mort's little shop.

Elena takes the vampire book from my hand and tosses it back onto the pile. "By being awesome," she says.

"Speaking of awesome . . ." I lift a copy of *To Kill a Mockingbird* off another display table.

Michael looks uncomfortable.

"What's wrong?" I ask him.

"Lucy," he says. "*To Kill a Mockingbird* is not my favorite book in the world."

"What's wrong with it?"

"It's about a little white tomboy who worships her father in a town filled with whacky racist Christians and lynch-mob farmers. It's a comedy about old-timey southern people who treat each other badly. It's—"

"That is not what it's about," I say.

"Actually," says Elena, "it sort of is."

"Not only that," Michael continues, "the big hero in the book is Atticus Finch, who is supposed to be some kind of super lawyer. But three of his clients end up getting executed, and he lets one murderer go free on purpose."

"Atticus Finch is not a hero because he's a good lawyer," I tell Michael. "He's a hero because he's a good man."

"He could have been better."

"Michael," I say, "we could all be better."

Based on the uncomfortable glances we're getting from nearby shoppers, I guess we've raised our voices more than a little. Elena steps between us. "How about we have a big argument about it in class when school starts in the fall?" she says. "That way we won't get kicked out of the mall today."

"Fine," I say.

"Fine," says Michael.

But I can't help adding one more thing. "If Mr. Nowak were still here, *To Kill a Mockingbird* would be our entire summer reading list."

"As if everybody in our class would actually read the book," Elena says.

"Everybody would have read it for Mr. Nowak," I tell her.

Elena shakes her head. "That's not going to happen now."

The three of us go back to flipping through the books on the display tables. Standing there with a hundred different mysteries and histories and adventures and literature at my fingertips, I remember what Mort said about the power of books and the power of bookstores. "What if we could make it happen?" I say.

Elena and Michael stop their browsing and look at me.

"What if we could make everybody read *To Kill a Mockingbird* this summer?" I ask them.

"How would we do that?" says Michael.

"I don't know," I admit. "We'd probably have to trick people into it."

"It would be an excellent way to remember Fat Bob," says Elena.

"It would," says Michael, "but—"

I interrupt before he can voice any objections. "Let's look around and see if we can come up with some ideas."

"What kind of ideas?" he asks.

"How do I know?" I say. "We haven't had them yet."

I turn and head toward the escalator that leads to the second floor. A moment later, we're riding the moving stairway. "So," says Elena, "it looks like we're heading to romance."

"Excuse me?" I say.

She points toward a big sign hanging above us. "It says so right there."

She's right. According to the sign, we are heading to the romance section.

"I like romance," Elena says.

"I thought you liked historical fiction," says Michael.

"That too." She turns to me. "What about you, Lucy?"

I feel my face burn red. "Shut up," I whisper.

"I'm just asking a question. You can tell because of the question mark at the end of my sentence."

"Stop it," I say under my breath.

"I can't stop something that you haven't started," she whispers.

I lean toward Elena and bump her with my hip. "I'm serious."

I'm just about to step off the escalator when Elena bumps me back. "Me too."

I know she doesn't mean to, but Elena's push throws me off balance. I misjudge the moving escalator steps and trip over my own feet. "Hey!" I shout.

Elena grabs for my arm, but instead of stopping me she shoves me toward a small table covered in books. I plow into it like a tall, skinny bulldozer. The table tips and knocks into a couple low shelves. Books fly everywhere. The next thing I know, I'm sitting on the floor surrounded by paperbacks covered with artistic renderings of pirates and ball gowns and big-busted ladies wearing looks of despair. I pick up one of the books and study the cover. "This is romance?"

Elena rushes forward. "I'm sorry! I didn't mean it. Are you all right?"

Michael joins us. "What happened?"

I get to my feet. "It was an accident. I'm fine."

I bend down and pick up a couple books. "We better clean this up."

That's when a small, balding man starts shouting from across the store. "Stop! Stop it!"

I sigh. "Now what?"

The man's name tag flaps up and down against a light blue shirt pocket while he runs. "Please stop!"

"Stop what?" Elena asks him.

The man slows to a halt, puts his hands on his knees, and doubles over to catch his breath. "I saw what happened. I'm the manager. Are you all right?"

I feel my face turn red again. I nod. "I'm okay."

"Thank goodness!" Even when he stands up, the top of the manager's head barely reaches my chin. The tag on his shirt says that his name is Mr. Dobby, and that he is associate manager for store number 389.

Elena steps forward. The manager is just her size, which makes Elena seem even more confident than usual. "Mr.—?"

"Dobby," he says. "It rhymes with Bobby."

Elena considers this. "We are really sorry about the mess, Mr. Dobby," she finally tells him. "We'll help clean it up."

Michael and I start collecting books again.

Mr. Dobby waves his hands above his head. "No!"

Elena puts her own hands up like she's being robbed. "What's wrong?"

"You don't know how to shelve books!" All of Mr. Dobby's statements seem like they should end in exclamation marks.

"Actually," says Elena, "we do."

Mr. Dobby shakes his head. "Shelving books incorrectly is as good as stealing them. It's almost worse. Our computers will show that we have a title in stock, but nobody will be able to find it. Not only that, it's very difficult to convince our corporate headquarters to send us a book if our computer insists that it's somewhere in the store." He lowers his voice. "Shelving badly leads to shrinkage."

"Shrinkage?" I say.

"Loss of profit due to loss of product," he explains. "Shrinkage is very, very bad." He takes a book from Elena's hand. "I know you're trying to help, and it is much appreciated, but you helped enough already." He pulls a couple coupons from his shirt pocket and shoves them into our hands. "Here," he tells us. "I'm just glad nobody got hurt. Now go visit our coffee bar and treat yourself to Mucho Mocha Creamo Cafiotta."

"DeCreamo what?" says Michael.

"They're my favorite!" says Mr. Dobby.

"Are they decaf?" asks Elena.

"Good heavens, no!"

"Wait a minute," I say. "If we take—" I grab a random paperback off the floor and read its title. "—*The Assyrian Pirate's Stentorian Housekeeper*, and we put it in the travel section instead of . . ."

"That belongs in Historical Romance," Mr. Dobby says knowingly.

"But if we shelve the pirate book next to—" I take a paperback off a nearby shelf and reads its title. "—*How to See Kalamazoo on Five Cents a Day*."

Mr. Dobby's eyes go wide. "We might never see that pirate again!"

"Really?" I say.

"Really," says Mr. Dobby. He takes the books away from Elena and me. "It's best to let a professional handle this."

"Okay, then." I hold up my coffee coupon. "Thank you for the special offer, Mr. Dobby."

He gives us a big smile. "I hope you found what you were looking for today!"

"We did," I tell him.

Elena turns to me. "We did?"

"Definitely," I say.

"Definitely?" asks Michael.

I turn back to Mr. Dobby. "Bye now!"

It's all I can do to keep myself from sprinting out of the store.

# 8
# Conspiracy Theories and Cruel Mistresses

. . . . . . . . . . . . . .

*The three of us huddle around a plastic table inside the* mall's food court. The area is decorated in dull tones of red and yellow and blue and green. Some kind of rowdy Irish-sounding music plays through speakers hidden behind the plastic trees while people wait in line for pizza and tacos and Mongolian stir fry. I grab a nacho from the paper basket between us and wave it around like I'm conducting a very tiny orchestra. "We are going to turn *To Kill a Mockingbird* into forbidden fruit!"

Michael turns to Elena. "Do you know what she's talking about?"

"All I know," says Elena, "is that she had two of those tall mucho caffeine things, and that can't be good."

"I'm fine!" I say, but I do feel a little wild-eyed. "Here's the thing. We are going to take copies of *To Kill a Mockingbird*, and we are going to make them disappear!"

"That's called stealing," says Michael.

I shake my head. "We're not going to steal."

"What are we going to do?" Elena asks.

I lower my voice. "Creative shelving. The books will never leave the store. We just put them in the wrong place."

"According to Mr. Dobby," says Michael, "that's as good as stealing."

"Except that it's not stealing," I say. "It's shrinkage."

Michael takes a nacho chip and points it at me. "When I see a bird that walks like a duck and swims like a duck and quacks like a duck, I call that bird a duck."

"Why are you talking about ducks?" Elena asks him.

Michael pops the chip into his mouth. "Because Lucy is talking about stealing."

"I'm talking about shrinkage," I say.

"Why are we talking about this at all?" asks Michael.

"Because of capitalism!" I say loudly.

A couple food court diners turn our way. They look a little worried. Maybe they're afraid that we're about to initiate an Occupy Wall Street movement right here at the mall.

"I don't think you need any more of those coffee drinks," Michael says to me.

"I'm still confused," says Elena.

"Capitalism is basic supply and demand," I explain. "If we lower the *To Kill a Mockingbird* supply—"

"Through creative shelving," says Elena.

I nod. "That will increase the demand."

"Fewer books will be available," Elena says slowly, "so more people will want books?"

"Exactly." I dip a chip into a puddle of hot sauce.

"Excuse me," says Michael, "that's not the way it works.

Capitalism requires the free flow of goods, and low supply does not increase demand. It—"

I cut him off. "Thank you, Karl Marx."

"I'm just saying—"

"I'm just saying that if people think that To Kill a Mockingbird is disappearing, they're going to want to get their own copies."

"No they're not," says Michael.

"Haven't you ever been to a grocery store before a snowstorm?" I ask him. "Everybody stocks up on bread and milk because they're afraid there won't be enough."

"Books are not the same as bread and milk," says Michael.

Elena wipes her face with a rough, brown napkin. "I could survive a snowstorm without milk, but that's because I'm lactose intolerant."

"What's your point?" Michael asks her.

"I think Lucy's point is that people will want what they think they can't have," Elena tells him.

"Just because something is missing doesn't mean people will want it," Michael replies.

"Making books disappear is just the first step," I say. "In fact, it's the easy part. The hard part will be getting the word out. We need people to think that To Kill a Mockingbird has been banned or something."

"You know what would be better?" says Elena. "If we could make people think that there's some kind of conspiracy to keep the book out of circulation."

"What?" says Michael.

"Seriously," says Elena. "Conspiracy theories are great for sales."

"There will be a conspiracy!" I say. "The conspiracy is us! Think about it. If you believed there was some kind of plot to keep a book out of your hands, wouldn't you want to read it?"

Neither Michael nor Elena responds.

"Of course you would!" I tell them. "Wanting what you can't have is the American way! All we have to do is make people think that they can't have *To Kill a Mockingbird*, and they'll be busting down the doors to get it."

Elena grins. "It will be like Charles Darwin's mobs at the boat docks."

"Charles Dickens," says Michael.

"Whatever," says Elena.

Michael shakes his head. "This is ridiculous. Even if we got rid of every book in the mall, you could still buy a copy from somewhere else."

"But what if we hid books in other stores, too?" I ask him.

"I could go to the library," says Michael.

"And if all the library books are gone?"

"I'd order it online."

"But in the meantime you'd have learned that the books are missing from everywhere else. You'd discover that there's some kind of mysterious plot going on that's supposed to prevent you from reading *To Kill a Mockingbird*. As a result, you'd really want to read it."

"But the plot will have failed," says Michael. "I got the book. I'll read it. You lose."

"No," says Elena. "In the end, you did what she wanted

you to do. You read *To Kill a Mockingbird*. Lucy wins!" She turns to me. "I like it."

The sane part of my brain knows that this whole thing is absurd. But honestly, I like it too. "Let's give it a try," I say.

"Let's not," says Michael.

Elena leans forward. "You'd do it for Newman Noggs."

Newman Noggs is a character in the novel *Nicholas Nickleby* by Charles Dickens. In fact, Noggs is one of Michael's very favorite characters. I can't believe that Elena remembers this.

"My mother is a police officer!" Michael reminds us.

"We're not breaking any laws," I say.

"I don't even like the book!" he protests.

"You like it enough," Elena tells him.

"And one day," I add, "you might want us to help you rescue Mr. Noggs."

"That's not fair!" he says.

Elena grins. "Literature is a cruel mistress."

Michael puts his head down on the food court table. "Why do I hang out with you two?"

"Because you are an independent thinking person who chooses his friends wisely," Elena says to Michael.

"We're going to be like terrorists," he says.

"We are not terrorists," I tell him. "We're more like literary saboteurs."

"Literary terrorists sounds better," offers Elena.

"My mother will kill me if she ever finds out about this. Actually," he adds, "she'll kill us all."

"Michael," I say, "it's not like we're starting a riot. We're encouraging people to read."

"You just said we're literary terrorists!"

"Michael," says Elena, "this isn't terrorism. This is community service. If we can pull it off, we'll probably get a medal."

Michael lifts his head off the table. "I bet that's what all the terrorists say."

# 9
# Always Look on the Bright Side of Life

. . . . . . . . . . . . . . .

*The next morning, I find Mom at the picnic table on our* back porch. She's got a sketch pad, a coffee cup, and a pile of colored pencils spread out in front of her. Photography is not the only thing she does well. She paints and sculpts. She plays piano and guitar. She writes poetry that she never lets anybody read. But her favorite thing of all is drawing. With a stubby pencil and a scrap of paper, my mother can take things she sees in her head and make them come alive.

I grab some yogurt and a spoon then open the sliding glass door that leads from the kitchen to the backyard. Mom lifts her head when I step onto the porch. "Hey, Lucy."

I wave my breakfast at her. "Good morning."

She points at my spoon. "Can I get one of those with a bowl of Fruit Loops?"

"No," I tell her. "You need healthy food."

She rolls her eyes.

I look down at her pad. The page is covered with quick sketches of robins and chickadees and blue jays. I like to draw, but I'll never be that good. Mom shows me her paper. "These are just the ones I saw this morning."

In addition to everything else, Mom is a birder. She can identify just about any species that's ever visited the eastern United States. She recognizes most of their songs, too.

I point at a few stray lines near the top of her page. "What's that?"

"It's supposed to be a crow. He flew away before I could get it right." Mom chooses a few pencils from the bunch on the table. She adds a purple smudge, some orange dots, and a couple sharp lines to the scribble. Now there's a jaunty black bird flying across her sheet. "There he is."

"How did you do that?" I ask.

Mom laughs. "His parts were there. I just had to fit them together."

That reminds me of something that Mr. Nowak used to say. "We are all broken, but sometimes the jagged pieces fit together nicely." I steal a glance at Mom's face. She doesn't look broken anymore.

"Are you going to sit?" asks Mom. "Or are you just going to stand there and stare at me?"

I sit.

Mom rips a blank page from her notebook. "Draw," she says.

"Draw what?"

A sharp *rat-tat-tat-tat* echoes off the trees around us.

"A woodpecker," says Mom. She grabs a dark pencil and starts to sketch.

I turn my head back and forth, but I don't see the bird. "Where is he?"

"Just see him in your head."

"I'd rather see him in a tree."

"It's probably a downy woodpecker. He's a little guy. White chest. Black-and-white wings. A mask on his face like a raccoon. The males have a bit of red on the tops of their heads. They're very dashing."

I look at the branches around us. "I still don't see him."

Mom points at a tall evergreen leaning toward our house. "Pretend that he's on a limb near the trunk. Draw what you'd see if he was sitting right there."

"But—"

"Just try."

I glance around one more time. I still can't find the woodpecker, so I lean over my paper and make a stick figure drawing of a bird.

"Don't forget to look at the tree," Mom says.

"But there's no woodpecker there."

"You have to pretend that there is."

I stay focused on my drawing. "Pretend that I'm pretending."

"Pretend that I'm not going to stick a pencil in your eye if you don't look into the branches."

I lean back and stare at the empty tree. "I think he's coming into view."

"Happy to hear it." Mom continues drawing while I continue glancing back and forth between the tree and my paper. Every once in a while, the air fills with the sound of his drumming. *Rat-tat-tat-tat* . . .

Mom smiles. "We hear you."

She never looks happier than when she is drawing. In fact, she says that her sketchbooks made as big a difference during her cancer treatments as the pain medicine that the doctors gave her. Even at her sickest, she tried to create at least one drawing every single day. Sometimes she drew stuff out of her head. Other times, she sketched nurses and orderlies and other patients. Once, she was so tired that she could barely sit up, but she struggled through a detailed drawing of her own scrawny fingers holding a pencil.

"You could take a day off," I told her then.

"I can't," she whispered.

"Why not?"

"I want to be an artist."

"You are an artist."

"Artists make art."

Now, Mom adds small details to her woodpecker so that the feathers on its head look like a messy crown. "You should write a book," I say.

"About what?" she asks.

"How to fight cancer with colored pencils."

Mom doesn't looks up. "Who says I was fighting cancer?"

"What do you mean?" I ask.

"Lucy," Mom says, "I'm not one of those people who think that cancer is some kind of jousting match. People live or die based on good medicine, good luck, and the grace of God. The people who die from it did not fail. The people who live will die another day."

My chest fills with a sudden, familiar pressure. I do not know how many times my heart has been broken and remade during this last year. "I'm glad you didn't die," I say.

"I'm glad too," Mom says, "but there were some days that death was the only thing that kept me going."

I look up. "I don't understand."

Mom turns her face to me. "Just so we're clear, being sick did not make me want to die."

"Okay."

"But it sure made me want to stop being sick. I figured that if I didn't get better, at least I would die and then I wouldn't feel so rotten anymore. One way or another, there was a light at the end of the tunnel."

"I guess that's one way of looking at it."

"Always look on the bright side of life, Lucy. And anyway, it's not like death is the end of the world."

"You mean heaven?" I ask.

"I mean people die every day, and the world is still spinning." Mom takes my paper and turns it around to study it. "That's a good thing."

"Are you talking about life, death, or my bird?"

"Life is good. Death is a mystery. The bird needs work."

I take my paper, turn it over, and try again. This time, I don't bother looking at the trees or at Mom or anything. I just draw what's on my mind. When I'm done, a little black bird sits on my page. It's more like a cartoon than the realistic drawings that Mom makes, but it's lively and confident and I like it.

"Nice," says Mom.

"Really?" I ask.

She nods. "What kind of bird is it?"

"Does it matter?" I ask.

"If it's art, then everything matters."

I stare down at my drawing. "It's a mockingbird."

# 10
# I Kill the Mockingbird

. . . . . . . . . . . . . . .

*After lunch, I tuck my mockingbird sketch into a back* pocket and let Mom know that I'm going to head to the bookshop for the afternoon.

"Look both ways before you cross the street," she tells me.

I start to protest, but then it strikes me that if I am very lucky I will be able to offer annoying safety tips to my own children one day. "I'll look both ways if you eat some fruit."

"Do strawberry Peeps count?"

"Strawberries would be good."

Mom grins. Her eyes are bright and lively, and her cheeks are filling out. I wish she'd eat a little better than she does, but her main food groups have always been coffee, candy, and fast food. "Lucy," she says, "Peeps make me happy, and happiness cures cancer."

"That's not what you said before."

"Peeps cure cancer!" Mom hollers as I head out the door.

When I arrive at the bookstore, Elena and Mort are

redecorating the display window that looks out onto Main Street. From the sidewalk, I see them assembling a stubby, fake Christmas tree next to a life-size Santa Claus doll that they've shoved into an old-fashioned school desk.

"What do you think they're doing?"

I turn and find Michael right beside me. He's wearing a pin-striped baseball uniform with grass stains on the elbows and knees. I'm guessing he already played today. I point to the green and red banner on the wall behind Santa. It says CHRISTMAS IN JULY.

"Ho, ho, ho," says Michael.

"How was your game?" I ask.

"We got beat, but I did okay in the field. I got on base once, and I struck out twice."

"You struck out?"

Michael smiles and nods. "These guys are good!"

"It's funny that striking out makes you happy."

"The best hitters in baseball can strike out two out of every three times they're at bat. Striking out doesn't make me happy, but you can't let it get you down. It's just part of the game."

"That's a good attitude."

"Plus," he says, "even if I were unhappy, that would change when I saw you."

I feel my face get very warm, and I expect my cheeks are about to turn bright red. "Thanks."

This would probably be a good moment for Michael and me to talk, but I suddenly feel like I've lost the ability to form coherent thoughts and sentences.

"Want to go inside?" Michael asks.

"Yes," I say. "Sure. Okay."

Michael looks at me oddly. "Okay."

There are no shoppers inside the bookstore at the moment, so Mort has the music turned up loud. He's got the place wired up with an old-style record player and a stereo system that includes several large, boxy speakers mounted to the ceiling. Now, a vinyl album is spinning on the turntable. A huge wall of sound filled with funky horns, an orchestral string section, some massive drums, and a set of jingle bells roar out of the speakers along with an all-girl chorus singing in perfect harmony.

> *Sleigh bells ring, are you listening?*
> *In the lane, snow is glistening.*
> *A beautiful sight,*
> *We're happy tonight.*
> *Walking in a winter wonderland . . .*

Mort sticks his head out from the doorway that leads to the window display space. "I love the holidays!"

I look over his shoulder. Elena is putting twinkly, red lights on the plastic tree. "I can tell," I shout over the music.

Mort turns down the volume. "I'm hoping that a little bit of Christmas will get some shoppers in here. We've hardly even sold any of your summer reading list books. I thought we'd go through a couple dozen of those by now."

"Sorry," I say.

He points at a stack of *To Kill a Mockingbird* copies. "There's only one thing keeping me from boxing those up and sending them back as returns."

"What's that?" I ask.

"It's a sin to kill a mockingbird."

That makes me laugh. It's one of the novel's most famous lines. In fact, I can recite that entire passage from memory. So I do. "Mockingbirds don't do one thing but make music for us to enjoy. They don't eat up people's gardens, don't nest in corncribs, they don't do one thing but sing their hearts out for us. That's why it's a sin to kill a mockingbird."

"That was your teacher's favorite part of the book," Mort tells me.

"Miss Caridas?"

Mort shakes his head. "Fat Bob."

"Really?"

Mort nods. "He thought the author was making a joke because real mockingbirds are territorial and aggressive. They'll peck an intruder to death if it gets too close to their nest. And as far as singing their hearts out, they do that by stealing other birds' songs."

"If that's the case, then there are a lot of characters in that novel who act like real mockingbirds," says Michael.

"But in the book," I say, "the mockingbird is supposed to be a symbol of innocence. That's why it's a sin to kill one."

"Who says it's a symbol of innocence?" asks Mort.

"Teachers," I tell him. "Book reviewers, critics—"

"Wikipedia," Elena calls from behind the display window.

"Everybody," I say.

"Maybe everybody is wrong," says Michael.

"They're not wrong," says Mort.

Elena steps out of the display window and joins us in the

shop. She turns to her uncle. "You said that mockingbirds are mean, selfish, hostile, thieving liars. Now you're saying they're not. Which is it?"

"Mockingbirds are creatures without a sense of right and wrong," Mort says. "That makes them innocent. They also behave exactly the way they were raised to behave. That means they are thieving, selfish, hostile liars. They can be innocent and wicked at the same time."

"That's not a joke," says Michael.

"Michael," says Mort, "contradiction and paradox are the building blocks of great humor."

"So is the mockingbird a symbol of innocence or not?" asks Elena.

Mort rolls his eyes. "Forget about symbols. *To Kill a Mockingbird* is not about symbols. It's about people."

"It's about selfish, hostile, thieving liars who might be innocents," says Elena.

Mort nods. "That's what Mr. Nowak would say."

"I think it's a story about growing up," I say, "and leaving things behind."

"It's about a lot of things," says Mort. "Mr. Nowak thought it should have been titled *HOW to Kill a Mockingbird*."

"I like that," says Elena.

"The book's original title was *Atticus*," he adds.

"I don't like that," says Elena.

"Harper Lee changed it at the last minute."

Elena shrugs. "Better late than never."

Mort glances at an ancient grandfather clock he's got propped in the corner. "Speaking of late, it's five minutes past lunchtime. You three watch the store while I go make us some sandwiches." He turns away then trots upstairs.

While we're waiting, I retrieve the mockingbird drawing from my back pocket and spread it out on the counter so that Elena and Michael can see. "What do you think?" I ask.

"That's excellent," says Michael.

"You really think so?"

He nods. "I do."

Elena stands behind him and makes kissy faces at me.

"Shut up," I say.

"What?" says Michael.

"Not you."

He turns to face Elena.

She gives him an innocent look. "I want to borrow Lucy's drawing for a second."

"Fine," I say.

She takes the sketch and brings it to the desktop copier near Mort's computer. She hits a button, and now there are two drawings. She gives the original back to me then takes a thick, black marker. "What if we do this?" she asks. Slowly and carefully, Elena draws a set of rings around the copy of my mockingbird. Now it looks like the bird is sitting at the center of a target. At the top of the page, Elena writes, HOW TO KILL A MOCKINGBIRD. Below the mockingbird's feet, she prints WWW.KILLaMOCKINGBIRD.com, then she pushes the paper back toward Michael and me. "There."

We both study the little poster. I take the marker. "May I?" I ask.

"Of course," says Elena.

When I'm done, the sign says, I KILL THE MOCKING-BIRD, and the web address is www.iKILLtheMOCKING BIRD.com.

Elena grins. "You're right. That's better."

"I kill the mockingbird?" Michael finally says.

"It's the name of our conspiracy," I tell him.

"All good conspiracies need a name," adds Elena.

"Is that so?" he asks.

"Area 51?" says Elena. "Watergate? Roswell? Fluoridation?"

Michael looks at me. "Do you know what she's talking about?"

"Mostly sometimes."

Michael just shakes his head.

I point to the web address below the mockingbird's feet. "How are we going to get a website?"

"How hard can it be?" says Elena.

Michael clears his throat. "I took a web design class at the community college last summer."

"Seriously?" I say.

"See," says Elena.

Above us, we hear Mort moving back toward the stairs. Elena leans forward and sticks a hand out in front of her as if we are in a huddle. "What do you say?" she asks Michael and me. "I kill the mockingbird?"

I place one hand on top of hers. "I kill the mockingbird," I say.

Michael glances back and forth between the two of us.

"Come on," I tell him.

"This is crazy," he says.

"No mockingbirds will be hurt in the making of this conspiracy," Elena promises.

Michael puts his hand over the top of mine. "I kill the mockingbird," he says, "but it's not the mockingbirds I'm worried about."

# 11
# Literary Terrorists Need Office Skills

. . . . . . . . . . . . . . .

*Over the next few days, I look for an opportunity to spend* some time alone with Michael, but between baseball games and helping Mom and working at the bookstore, we just don't get a chance.

In the meantime, Michael, Elena, and I are able to bike, bus, and walk to various libraries in West Glover, Windsor, Simsbury, Bloomfield, and a few others, too. We wander around the stacks, identify our targets, and then place *To Kill a Mockingbird* copies on new shelves where nobody will ever look. Back at the River Road Mall, we revisit Mr. Dobby's store and assign new locations to his books as well. In their places, we leave I Kill the Mockingbird flyers and then hope for the best. In fact, we use so many flyers that we're going to need more. That's why we sneak into the empty St. Brigid's School building while my dad is away for lunch.

"You're sure the building is empty?" Michael whispers. We are creeping up the stairwell that connects the basement cafeteria to the first floor. Our footsteps echo like drum-beats inside a cave.

"Positive," I say.

"Really positive?"

"For the millionth time," Elena growls at Michael, "she is absolutely certain. All the teachers are on vacation. The school secretary is away on a cruise. The janitor is in the hospital having cosmetic surgery."

"Back surgery," I correct her.

"Whatever," snaps Elena.

Michael stops at the doorway that leads into the main part of the building. "And the principal?"

Elena leans into the door, which swings wide open. She grabs Michael's sleeve and pulls him through. "He is at home having lunch with his lovely wife. We. Are. Alone." Elena punctuates the last three words by poking Michael in the chest. "Okay?"

"Okay," he says.

"Good. Because—" Elena is interrupted by a loud clatter and banging from somewhere nearby. "Somebody's coming!" she cries.

The three of us throw ourselves into the closest class-room. We scatter and hide behind anything we can find. I drop my backpack to the floor and squeeze beneath a fold-ing table while Elena tries to press herself against a wall. Michael ducks behind the teacher's desk at the front of the room. The three of us hold our breaths while we wait to see what happens next.

"A folding table is not a good hiding place," Elena finally whispers at me.

"It's better than a wall!"

"Shhhh!" says Michael. Of the three of us, he's the only one who's really concealed.

Elena edges toward one of the tall classroom windows and peaks outside. Her shoulders sag and she starts to laugh.

"What is it?" I say.

She points outside just as a big old garbage truck rolls past. "I don't think Majewski's Sanitation Service is after us."

Michael peeks his head around the side of the desk. "Are you sure that's what we heard?"

"I'm sure." Elena leads us out of the classroom and down the hallway toward the main office. When we get there, I pull Dad's set of spare keys out of my pocket and unlock the door. The three of us slip inside where I open my backpack and pull out an updated version of our flyer. I hold it up so that Michael and Elena can see.

"What do you think?"

The paper holds my stick figure mockingbird drawn on top of a black-and-white target. I also snipped letters from magazine titles and newspaper headlines to create a sort of ransom note. At the very bottom of the page, fat block letters spell out our web address.

"That's awesome," says Elena.

"I updated the website last night," says Michael.

"The links to Facebook and Twitter and Instagram all work?"

"I'm doing my best," he says. "It's not easy setting all this up under my mother's nose. If she finds out what we're up to, I am dead."

www.iKILLtheMOCKINGBIRD.com

"We're not breaking any laws," says Elena.

Michael gestures at the dark office around us. "We are breaking and entering. We are trespassing. We are about to use school office equipment in order to create an impression that West Glover has been targeted by a group of mysterious literary terrorists."

Elena grins. "When you put it like that, it sounds even better!"

"Let's just make our copies and get out of here." Michael

approaches the big duplicating machine against the back wall. "Do either one of you know how to turn this thing on?"

I join him and punch a couple buttons on the machine's front panel, but nothing happens.

"We are pitiful," he says.

Elena walks past us, reaches a hand behind the copier, and pushes a switch. The machine begins to hum and glow. "Speak for yourself."

I lift the cover and place the mockingbird poster onto the glass. "How many copies should we make?"

"Five hundred?" Elena suggests.

"Sounds good." I punch the number into the machine's keypad. Nothing happens so I punch in the numbers again. Still nothing.

"Now what?" asks Michael.

I glance around and notice a crucifix on the wall. "We could use a little help here," I say to Jesus.

"I can't believe you two." Elena reaches between us and pushes another button. A blue-green light glows beneath the copier lid. A moment later, mockingbird posters begin pouring out as if the machine is possessed by Gutenberg's ghost. Together, we start gathering copies and stuffing them into my bag. Soon, we've filled my backpack as well as a few plastic grocery bags we find laying around the office.

"I think we have enough," Michael says.

"This seems like more than five hundred." I glance at the clock on the wall. It is twelve fifty-five. My father will be back soon, and the machine is still going strong. "We really have to go."

"Uh oh," says Elena, who is staring down at the copy machine.

"What's wrong?" asks Michael.

"The machine isn't making five hundred copies. It's making five *thousand* copies!"

"How can that be?" I ask.

"Who punched in the numbers?"

Michael and I join Elena at the copier. According to the display, there are still several thousand copies to go. "We've got to stop it!" I say.

Michael points out the window. "We'd better stop it soon," he says, "because here comes your father."

I glance outside. Michael is right. Dad is heading toward the building from the parking lot. In a panic, I start punching random keys on the control panel. This time, there's a strange clacking and grinding noise. Now the machine is printing double-sided copies with two staples in each corner.

"That's pretty cool," says Elena.

"Shut it off!" I say.

Elena begins stuffing the new copies into anything that will hold them. Michael looks as if he's about to pass out.

"Do something!" I yell.

Michael looks up at the crucifix on the wall.

"Michael," says Elena, "Jesus does not know how to operate office equipment."

"He helped before!"

"Get out of the way." She ducks behind the machine and grabs the power cord. "Stand back!"

Michael and I move toward the door and Elena yanks

the plug out of the wall. There's a loud CLACK! and the machine sputters to a halt.

"Why did we have to stand back?" I ask.

Elena shrugs. "It seemed like the right thing to say."

I take a chance and look out the window. I don't see Dad on the sidewalk which means he must be about to enter the building. "We've got to go!"

The three of us gather up our things and head for the door. "Wait!" says Michael.

Elena is struggling with several plastic trash bags filled with mockingbird copies. "Now what?"

Michael doesn't answer. Instead, he races back into the office, lifts the copier lid, and whips the original poster off the glass. From there, he leads us into the hallway and pulls the office door shut behind us. The three of us sprint all the way back to the empty cafeteria where Michael hands me my artwork. "I didn't think you wanted to lose that."

I shake my head and try to catch my breath. "Thanks."

Elena plops into a plastic cafeteria chair. "I don't know about you," she says, "but I learned something new today."

"What did you learn?" Michael asks her.

"Literary terrorists need office skills."

# 12
# How to Eat an Elephant

. . . . . . . . . . . . . . .

**By mid-July, I Kill the Mockingbird is in full motion.** Thanks to cheap student passes for the transit buses that make hourly stops in West Glover, and because Connecticut is so small, we can get to almost any spot in our state and still be home for supper. "We'd never be able to pull this off in Texas," Michael says while we study maps and bus schedules in the back room at Mort's.

Elena points at the fancy seal stamped on one of our transit flyers. "This caper is made possible by the State Department of Transportation."

"That's our tax dollars at work," Michael adds.

Meanwhile, we've discovered that Connecticut is home to over six dozen bookstores and nearly three hundred public libraries. We've also learned that *To Kill a Mockingbird* is on sale at Target, Toys "R" Us, Sam's Club, Wal-Mart, Kmart, QuickMart, GasMart, DairyMart, MiniMart, and more. It's going to be impossible to hit them all. "We'll deal with it as if we are eating an elephant," Elena says.

"How do you eat an elephant?" asks Michael.

Elena gives him a big grin. "One bite at a time."

That makes us laugh.

"And remember," she adds, "we don't have to eat the whole thing. It only has to look that way."

"Just the same," I say, "we better get hungry."

We continue re-shelving the books in nearby libraries, and that's pretty easy. Local department stores are simple, too. We collect *To Kill a Mockingbird* copies then shove them behind auto supplies. "You're not looking for literature when you have car-care needs," says Elena.

"What makes you think that?" Michael asks her.

"Simple common sense," she explains.

Michael and I have known Elena long enough to understand that her common sense is rarely simple or common, so we don't argue.

At gift shops and grocery markets, we slip copies of *To Kill a Mockingbird* behind posters and planters and greeting card racks. We do the same at the giant bookstores that live inside our state's mega-malls. Connecticut is also home to about three dozen different college and university bookstores. They turn out to be the easiest targets of all. We simply place the books under baseball caps and football jerseys. I honestly don't know why the college shops aren't called sweatshirt stores that just happen to sell books on the side.

It's the small bookstores like Mort's that give us the biggest headaches. Those places believe in customer service and personal attention, which means that you can't get away with anything. More than once we end up actually buying books to avoid raising the owners' suspicions. Finally, so that we won't go broke, we admit that independent booksellers are just too smart for us, and we decide to leave most of them alone.

In the midst of our creative shelving efforts, we also place I Kill the Mockingbird flyers in as many locations as possible. We tuck them into the empty spots that used to hold all the books we've moved. We tack them onto community bulletin boards and tape them onto shop windows. We take our flyers and use them to wallpaper the state. And yet, despite all that, it hardly seems like anybody has even noticed our work.

Until now.

After a long day trying—and failing—to find a bookshop called Mark Twain's House, Elena brings us back to Mort's. Inside, Mort is getting ready to close up. "I'm glad we didn't find the place," Michael says as we head inside. "Mark Twain made black people look like buffoons."

Mort looks up. He doesn't know what we're talking about, but that doesn't stop him from joining the conversation. "Michael," says Mort, "Mark Twain made everybody look like buffoons. He was an equal opportunity buffoon maker."

Michael sighs. "I guess you're right."

Mort shuts his cash register. "I know I'm right."

"The king has spoken," says Elena. She turns toward her uncle. "Can we hang out in the shop for a while?"

"This is a place of business," Mort says. "It is not your own private clubhouse."

"We're going to listen to loud music, surf the Internet, eat junk food, and make plans to take over the world. We can do that upstairs in the apartment if you'd like."

"Don't stay up too late, and be sure to lock the door when you're done," Mort tells us.

Once he leaves, the three of us head to the computer. Elena fires up the machine while Michael flips through a set of vinyl records that Mort's got stacked beneath his desk. Michael finds a record he likes, places it on the turntable, and drops the needle onto the disk. A driving, bluesy harmonica blares from the big speakers, and a man with a deep, rough voice howls that he's got his mojo working.

"Check this out!" Elena hollers.

Michael and I look over her shoulder at the computer. Elena's got the screen split between several different social networking sites. We've created anonymous I Kill the Mockingbird accounts on all of them. In the top corner, she's also opened the web page we created at WWW.iKILLthe MOCKINGBIRD.com. That's anonymous, too.

"People are talking about us!" Elena announces.

"No way," I say.

"What are they saying?" asks Michael.

On Facebook, I Kill the Mockingbird's got several hundred Likes and bunches of comments. On Tumblr and Instagram, we find snapshots of our flyers; and on Twitter, we've become #ikillthemockingbird as in:

WHO STOLE MY MOCKINGBIRD? #ikillthemock-
ingbird

What's up with the mockingbird conspiracy? #ikillthemockingbird

This is a little scary and a lotta cool.
#ikillthemockingbird

FINALLY SOMEBODY'S GOT A GOOD IDEA FOR
MY SUMMER READING BOOKS! #ikillthemock-
ingbird

Michael points at that last comment. "That's not funny."

"How did it finally get started?" I wonder out loud.

Elena starts clicking and scrolling through snippets of conversations and posts.

It's a sin to kill a mockingbird.
#ikillthemockingbird

THIS IS A NOVEL HOSTAGE SITUATION!
HA.HA.HA. #ikillthemockingbird

"Whoa," says Michael.

"What is it?" I ask.

Michael shakes his head in disbelief. He points at the screen. "Wil Wheaton saw an I Kill the Mockingbird flyer and tweeted about it."

"Wil Wheaton?" I say.

"Wil Wheaton!" Michael says again. "Wil Wheaton!"

"Who is Wil Wheaton?"

"Wil Wheaton!"

"Michael," says Elena, "no matter how many times you say his name, we still don't know who you're talking about."

"He's a gamer!" Michael takes the mouse from Elena and

clicks on Wil Wheaton's profile. "He's a total geek hero! He's an author and an actor. He used to be on *Star Trek!*"

I point at the description that Wil Wheaton has written about himself. "It says here that he's just a guy."

"Just a guy who used to be on *Star Trek!*" says Michael.

I study the profile page more closely. "This guy has two-and-a-half million followers online!"

"Did I mention the *Star Trek?*" Michael asks.

"You mentioned it," I say.

"How did we get an I Kill the Mockingbird poster aboard the starship *Enterprise?*" asks Elena.

"We should reply," I say.

Michael's mouth drops open. "To Wil Wheaton?"

"To everybody."

"That's why it's called *social* networking," adds Elena.

"What would we say?" asks Michael.

"Thank you?" I suggest.

Elena thinks for a moment. "Now that people have noticed us, we've got to keep it going."

Outside, the sun is heading toward the horizon. A sliver of orange moon floats high in the summer sky. In the distance, red and white lights atop giant broadcast antennas blink on and off like gods that do not know we exist. I want people to know that we exist. "We can share the list of places that we've hit so far," I suggest.

"Do you want to get caught?" asks Michael.

"Or," I say, "we can list all our targets whether we've hit them or not. We want people to know that I Kill the Mockingbird is big—"

"—and that it's coming to your town soon!" says Elena.

Michael shakes his head. "I don't think that's a good idea."

Elena and I push him away from the computer then open the document containing our roster of Connecticut libraries, retailers, and booksellers. With a couple quick clicks, Elena pastes the list onto a new page called OUR TARGETS.

"Thanks for considering my input," says Michael.

"We considered it," says Elena. "And then we rejected it."

On the record player, a new song begins to play. According to the singer, he's been down so long that up don't make sense no more.

"From now on," Elena continues, "we reply to every note, every comment, and every tweet, and on all those replies, we add a link back to the OUR TARGETS page. We never say what the list is for. We never communicate directly with any of the targets. We just make sure that people know about it. Pretty soon they'll start thinking that they are all part of the conspiracy."

Michael throws his hands in the air. "Since it's just a list, why limit it to Connecticut? Why not tell the whole country that we're coming to get them?"

Elena and I both get stunned looks on our faces. "That's a great idea!" I say.

"I was kidding!" he says.

"If we're lucky," I say, "people will start to believe that this is huge!"

"What if we're not lucky?" asks Michael.

"The only way this thing works is if we get noticed," I tell him.

"We are creating a monster," Michael says.

Elena hunches over and rubs her hands together. "But it will be a very good monster!"

Michael shakes his head. I laugh out loud. "You sound like Dr. Frankenstein," I say to Elena.

"No," Elena replies. "This is what Dr. Frankenstein sounds like." She stands on her chair, pulls her hair into a crazy mess, and then screeches in her best horror movie voice, "IT'S ALIVE!"

"God help us," says Michael.

Elena goes back to the computer and starts to type. Michael and I stand behind her and read the various comments. Without thinking, I reach over and take Michael's hand in my own. "Don't worry," I tell him. "It's going to be all right."

Michael doesn't reply, but he doesn't pull away so we stand there, hand in hand, for a very long time. "Okay," he finally says to me. "I'll believe you."

# 13
# Patron Saint of the Blind

· · · · · · · · · · · · · ·

*Less than twenty-four hours later, I'm the one saying my* prayers. This time, I'm making my appeal to the tiny plastic St. Lucy statue that Dad keeps on the television set in our living room. My namesake is the patron saint of eye disorders, and her statue is supposed to remind us not to sit too close to the TV screen.

"This is not the kind of help Michael was talking about," I say to the saint.

St. Lucy doesn't look at me. She can't because she gouged out her own eyes to avoid marrying a pagan. In fact, images of St. Lucy always show her with two eyeballs on a tray. Our own Lucy statue holds a simple, silver platter. I used to think she was carrying two eggs over easy. Now I know that the whole Catholic thing can be seriously weird sometimes.

"Can you believe this?" shouts Elena. Her voice is loud and clear in the phone against my ear.

"I cannot believe this," I say.

On television, a reporter with a microphone stands beside a small man in front of a long bookshelf.

"It's Mister Dobby!" Elena screams.

"I know."

"MISTER DOBBY!" Elena yells again.

"He can't hear you," I say, but Elena does not reply.

On the screen, our old friend Mr. Dobby looks a little stunned. "According to store manager, Algar Dobby . . ." says a reporter who looks like an aging supermodel.

"Algar?" says Elena.

"Shhh!"

". . . it's not unusual to run low on a book like *To Kill a Mockingbird*." The picture cuts to a close-up of Mr. Dobby who is nodding like a bobble head doll. The reporter continues talking. "*To Kill a Mockingbird* is an American classic and a regular part of many schools' summer reading lists."

The camera cuts to Mr. Dobby. "We always make sure we have enough copies of books like that," he says. "But someone or some group has been working to sabotage that effort this summer."

"SABOTAGE?" yells Elena.

"Sabotage?" asks the reporter.

Mr. Dobby holds one of our flyers up to the camera. My mockingbird bull's-eye fills the television screen. "These ransom notes have been discovered throughout the store."

"Hold it so that we can see it!" Elena yells at the television.

As if he can hear us, Mr. Dobby lifts the sign a tiny bit higher so that the camera gets a better angle. Now, the whole thing—including our web address—is as clear as day.

"Thank you, Mr. Dobby!" shouts Elena.

"I kill the mockingbird dot com," says the reporter.

"Thank you, pretty reporter lady!" Elena adds.

The camera pulls away to show the reporter giving Mr. Dobby a serious look. "Do you think this is some kind of a threat?"

"I don't know what it is." The top of Mr. Dobby's head barely reaches the woman's chest. Beside her, he looks like a small, balding sixth grader. "But whoever is behind this should know that we have contacted all the proper authorities." He turns toward the camera. "Stealing books is against the law, and censorship is just plain un-American."

"You tell 'em, Mr. Dobby!" shouts Elena.

"Also," Mr. Dobby adds, "people should know that we will have every copy of *To Kill a Mockingbird* on sale for half off the regular price."

"Are copies of the book available now?" the reporter asks.

"No," says Mr. Dobby, "but they should be arriving soon."

"Not if we can help it!" says Elena.

The reporter stares straight into the camera. "If you have information in regards to who might be killing the mockingbirds, please call the Action News Hotline today. This is Dontine Flora reporting."

"Dontine?" says Elena.

"Lucy," Dad calls from the kitchen, "I could use some help in here."

"I've got to go," I whisper into the phone.

"This is awesome!" says Elena.

"It's something," I admit before I hang up.

In the kitchen, Dad fills a bowl with fresh greens and sliced tomatoes. Before Mom got sick, we were a mostly fast-food family. Now I can't remember the last time that Dad and I pulled supper out of a paper bag.

"How are your friends?" Dad asks while he places dishes on the table.

"Elena's fine," I tell him. "Michael had a baseball game today."

"I'm talking about Dontine Flora and Algar Dobby."

I don't reply.

"I couldn't help overhearing the news." Dad holds a spoon up to his face as if he's speaking into a microphone. "Hi," he says in a breathy voice, "I'm Dontine Flora reporting to you live from ground zero in the summer reading sabotage scandal." Dad lowers the utensil then reaches into his back pocket. He pulls out a folded piece of paper and hands it to me. I unfold the sheet and discover a torn, wrinkled version of the flyer that was on TV a moment ago.

"Look familiar?" Dad asks.

I study the paper. "I saw it on the news."

"This one was stuck inside the copy machine at school."

I say nothing.

"How do you think it got there?"

"That is a very good question."

"That is not really an answer."

Again, I choose silence.

Dad studies the flyer. "I kill the mockingbird," he says out loud. "It's a catchy slogan."

I take the salad bowl and carry it to the table.

"Do you want to tell me what's going on?"

"Not really," I say.

"Does it involve stealing books from Mr. Dobby?"

"Nobody is stealing," I promise.

Dad hands me a loaf of fresh bread then lifts a pot filled with gazpacho, which is a cool, tasty vegetable soup. "Have any laws been broken?"

"Not that I'm aware of."

"Has anyone put themselves into danger in any way?"

I place napkins and bowls on the table. "I don't think so."

"So making copies without permission is probably the worst of it."

"Probably."

"Probably?"

"Definitely."

"Lucy," says Dad, "I don't want this summer to end with me having to extricate you from the clutches of some mall cop."

As far as I know, there's not a mall within fifty miles that still has *To Kill a Mockingbird* copies in plain sight. "That's not going to happen," I promise.

"You're sure?"

"Positive."

"Good."

Together, the two of us finish setting the table. A moment later, Mom comes in through the door that leads from the kitchen to the garage. "Hi!" she says.

Dad points at a big white bag in her hand. "What's that?"

"Burgers and fries," she announces. "I'm starving!"

# 14
# Wanting Is an Act of Courage

. . . . . . . . . . . . . . .

*After a supper of greasy burgers and fries plus a healthy* soup and salad, I head to my room and text Michael. DID YOU SEE THE NEWS?

He responds a moment later. TV NEWS?

NO, I write back. SMOKE SIGNALS & SEMAPHORE.

I DON'T WATCH TV.

I happen to know that he's a huge fan of *Buffy the Vampire Slayer* reruns. YOU ARE A LIAR.

SAY THAT TO MY FACE.

WITH PLEASURE.

MEET ME IN FRONT OF YOUR HOUSE.

WHEN?

RIGHT NOW.

I look outside my window. Michael is sitting on the lawn with his bicycle beside him. I head downstairs and join him in the grass. "What are you doing here?"

He nods across the street toward his driveway. "I'm your neighbor."

I put my hands on my hips.

"And I'm locked out of my house."

"How did that happen?"

"I had a baseball game. I forgot my keys. My mom's not home from work yet. I was sitting on our front steps when you texted me."

"You are a liar."

"No." He points at his knee-high socks and pin-striped pants. "Really. It was a double-header."

"I believe you. I just want you to know I don't mind calling you a liar to your face. How was the game?"

"Two wins for us," he tells me.

"I don't care who won. I care about . . ." I'm about to say YOU, but then I realize how that might sound. Actually, it would sound a lot like the truth. "Did you get any hits? Any runs? Any homers?"

"No outs. A few hits."

"Home runs?"

"Four."

"You hit four home runs?"

He grins. "Two in the first game and two in the second."

"Maybe you really will play in the big leagues one day."

Michael finds a piece of clover and pulls it out of the grass. He gets uncomfortable when people talk about his baseball future. He just likes playing the game.

Around us, the neighborhood is settling into the quiet of a summer night that is really not that quiet at all. Crickets and toads chirp and peep. Someone nearby is practicing scales on an out-of-tune piano near an open window. A jangly ice-cream truck song plays in the distance. Michael points at a couple bats that swoop and whoosh through the trees above us. "It's hard to believe that they're blind."

I think of St. Lucy with her eyes on a plate.

"Sometimes," says Michael, "I feel like I could be blind and still hit anything a pitcher throws at me."

"How would you do that?"

"Every once in a while, when I'm standing at the plate, I start to feel really, really quiet. I almost feel invisible, but at the same time I can see and hear every single thing that's going on around me. The catcher flexing the leather on his mitt. The runner on first chatting with the first baseman because they used to be in cub scouts together. A squirrel dragging a popcorn box beneath the bleachers near the third baseline."

"You see all that?"

"It's not really seeing. It's more like knowing. By the time the pitcher steps into his windup, I know exactly what he's going to throw. I know where it's going to be over the plate. I know where the ball is going to connect on the bat. It's a sure thing. It's almost like I can see the future. Right then, I could close my eyes and hit anything out of the park."

"Have you ever tried it?" I ask. "Closed your eyes?"

Michael shakes his head. "Baseball is a team sport."

"So?"

"So playing with your eyes closed is not what teammates do."

"Even if it's a sure thing?"

Michael turns and looks into my face. The sun is low now and long shadows stretch across the neighborhood. "Even if it was a sure thing. That would take a pretty big leap of faith."

Suddenly, I think that we are not talking about baseball anymore. "I guess there are no sure things."

Michael doesn't respond. Part of me wishes that he'd just come out and say that he likes me. I mean, if he does like me, that's what he should say. But then again, maybe he doesn't like me. Not like that. Maybe Elena is wrong. And maybe I am going insane.

"Lucy," Michael says to me, "you have a really funny look on your face."

"Gee, thanks."

He laughs which makes me laugh too. "What were you thinking?"

"I was thinking—" I hesitate. "You know," I tell him, "sometimes I don't know what I want."

He nods as if he is agreeing with me, but then he says, "I don't believe you."

"What?"

"You always know what you want."

"I do not."

"Sometimes you just don't want to say what you want. There's a difference."

I don't reply.

"You're doing it right now."

I still don't speak.

"According to my baseball coaches, everything is about wanting. They always say, 'You have to *want* it.' You have to want to win. You have to want to get a hit. You have to want to make the catch. You spend a whole game wanting." He shakes his head. "Another definition of wanting is to be missing something."

"I never thought of it like that," I say.

"When you want something," says Michael, "it's like admitting that your life has a hole in it."

"And to fill that hole, you need something that you don't have and you might not get."

Michael gives a little laugh. "I never thought of it like that."

I recall a lesson from our world religions class. "Didn't the Buddha say that wanting is what makes people suffer?"

"The Buddha didn't play baseball," says Michael.

"If he did, maybe he'd think that wanting isn't such a bad thing."

Michael nods. "In some ways, I think that wanting is an act of courage."

"What do you mean?"

He shakes his head. "I don't know exactly, but it's okay if you don't want to say what you want, Lucy. You're one of the bravest people I know. You'll say it eventually."

Michael's words take me by surprise. They are so kind. Even if they're not true. "I'm not brave."

Michael reaches over and puts his hand on mine. His palm is rough and warm. "You saved your mom's life. I think you saved your dad, too. That was brave."

I think back on the days and weeks and months of running from doctor to doctor. At first, I wanted to cry all the time. But then, I just decided that tears would not be helpful. Keeping the house clean, on the other hand, that was helpful. Learning how to cook, that was helpful, too. And getting better grades than usual so that Mom and

Dad would have one less thing to worry about . . . I think it made a small difference.

I lean into Michael a little bit. "I couldn't have done it without Elena and you."

Michael takes my hand and gives it a squeeze. "We know it."

Headlights from a passing car sweep over us, and we pull away from each other. It's Michael's mom pulling her police cruiser into their driveway.

"I'd better go," Michael says.

We both stand. "Don't you want me to tell you about the news?" I ask.

"I almost forgot," he says.

"Mr. Dobby was on TV. Apparently, there's some kind of conspiracy to keep people from reading *To Kill a Mockingbird*."

"You don't say?"

"I do say."

Michael lifts his bike off the ground then swings a leg over the seat. He must not be paying attention to what he's doing because he nearly loses his balance. I reach out and put a hand on his shoulder to steady him. Suddenly, we are very close together again.

"Thanks," says Michael.

"You should be careful," I tell him.

"Okay," he says.

"Okay," I say.

He doesn't reply. I guess our conversation has become just too scintillating.

"I should go," he says once more.

"Okay," I say again. If only somebody was passing out hundred dollar bills in exchange for one word answers tonight . . .

He glances at his shoulder. "But you'll have to let go of my arm."

"Right." I release him and step back.

"See you tomorrow, Lucy." A couple of quick strokes on the pedals send Michael across the street. Heading into the house, he raises an arm and waves at me without looking back. I'm left standing alone in the grass. Inside, I feel a small, warm hope begin to glow.

# 15
# Where Is Elena Going with That Ax?

. . . . . . . . . . . . . . .

**When I get to the bookshop the next day, Michael and** Elena are huddled near the store's back wall. Mort looks up from his computer when I enter. "Have you heard about this I Kill the Mockingbird thing?" he asks me.

I hesitate, but then Elena steps up before the silence goes on for too long. "It's been on the news."

Mort grunts and points to his tabletop display featuring summer reading choices for all our local schools. "Why hasn't anybody stolen my books?"

"Excuse me?" I say.

"This is an awesome publicity opportunity," Mort continues. "I don't want to miss it."

"Well," I say after an awkward silence, "it's probably not over yet."

Michael approaches the front of the store. "Shut up!" he whispers at me.

"What do you mean?" Mort asks.

"I—"

Elena interrupts me. "On the news they made it sound like it's an ongoing thing. Maybe we'll get lucky and somebody will break into our store."

Michael grabs a random book and pretends to flip through it. "Where did you hear about I Kill the Mockingbird?" he asks Mort.

"Booksellers' chat room," Mort explains. "It's on the computer."

Michael tries to be nonchalant as he puts *What to Expect When You're Expecting* back on a shelf. "What exactly are they saying?"

Mort waves his hand dismissively. "Everybody's got a theory. It's mostly nonsense. Some people are yelling that this is a blow against free speech. Others think it's a conspiracy by e-book sellers. It might just be a simple publisher inventory problem, or it's a publicity campaign that's remarkably stupid or unbelievably brilliant." Mort shakes his head. "A few people think it's just a big practical joke, but I don't see how that's possible."

"Why not?" I ask.

"It's too widespread. I think I'm the only store in Connecticut that still has *To Kill a Mockingbird* in stock."

Elena shakes her head. "That's not true."

"How do you know?" says Mort.

"She means it CAN'T be true," says Michael. "How could it be?"

Mort shrugs. "There are even reports from stores in other states that copies have gone missing."

"Other states?" I say.

Mort nods. "I've heard that stores in Massachusetts and Rhode Island have been hit."

It actually wouldn't be that difficult for us to get to those states. It's only about ninety minutes by bus from West Glover to Boston or Providence. Even New York City is only about two hours away. But we haven't been anywhere outside of Connecticut.

Mort heads back to his desk and plops into the chair. "How am I going to get in on this?"

Michael, Elena, and I put our heads together. "What's happening?" I say.

"Copycats," Michael whispers. "People are talking about it online. They saw Mr. Dobby and Dontine Flora on the TV news. They're trying to get their own local *Mockingbird* heists on TV, too."

"Did you tell them they're not actually supposed to steal the books?" I ask.

"How am I supposed to do that without giving us away?"

"What are you three talking about?" says Mort.

Elena turns to her uncle. "We think we can help."

"We do?" says Michael.

Elena nods. "Follow me."

A moment later, we're dragging big, plastic bins from the shop's back room. The boxes hold the holiday supplies that Mort uses to decorate throughout the year. "It's already Christmas in July," he reminds us.

"And Santa will continue to lead the way," Elena tells him. She directs us toward the display area where Jolly Old Saint Nick is sitting beside his tree. "Who's got the Halloween box?"

Michael points at a skull and crossbones label on the side of a bin. "Is this it?"

Elena pops the lid off the container. She reaches into the box and pulls out a huge fake hatchet that's covered in Halloween blood.

"What is that for?" Michael asks.

Elena pulls the ax out of the bag, holds it above her head, and shouts, "I KILL THE MOCKINGBIRD!"

Michael shakes his head. "I am seriously worried about you."

"This will be great publicity for Mort." Elena lowers her voice. "And it lets us hide in plain sight."

"I hope you know what you're doing," he says.

"Michael," I whisper, "she knows just as much as we do." Michael sighs. "We are so doomed."

"Mort," Elena calls to her uncle. "Do we have a hardcover version of *To Kill a Mockingbird?*"

"I saw one yesterday," I say. "I'll get it." I head to the used fiction section and browse the shelves until I find the book I'm looking for. The cover is old and wrinkled and mostly gray. The author's name—Harper Lee—appears in bold, white letters above the title. Below, a pen-and-ink drawing of a dead mockingbird lies on its back. It's surrounded by blood-red strands of ivy.

I return to Elena and hand her the book. "Perfect!" she says.

"For what?" asks Mort.

"You'll see," she promises.

"Where is Elena going with that ax?" Michael mutters.

"Very funny," Mort tells him.

We follow Elena into the display area where Santa, still squished into the school desk, stares blankly out the window. Red and green Christmas lights decorate the tree and the walls around him. Several stacks of old books and magazines rest neatly at Santa's feet.

"You've got to trust me," Elena says to Mort.

"Okay," he says. "I trust you."

"Here we go then." Elena takes a quick step toward one of the book piles and kicks it into the wall. The books scatter everywhere.

"Hey!" Michael hollers.

"What are you doing?" I shout.

"Decorating," Elena explains. She tips over a nearby bookshelf then yanks the Christmas lights off the wall. She lifts a pile of old National Geographics and throws them into the air. The magazines flutter around us like giant, yellow moths. In just a few seconds, Elena has turned Christmas in July into the aftermath of a home invasion. But she's not done yet. "Give me the book," she instructs me.

I look at the disaster around us then hide the novel behind my back.

She points at me with her ax. "Hand it over, Lucy."

I love *To Kill a Mockingbird*, but I'm not the sort of person who says no to a bloody hatchet. I give Elena the book.

"Thank you." She turns away from me then heads to Santa. Somehow, she secures his black-mittened hand to the hatchet's handle. From there, she props *To Kill a Mockingbird* on Santa's school desk. Then she sinks the Halloween blade into the pages of the book so that it looks like Santa is trying to dismember the great American novel. "HO

101

HO HO!" Elena says in a big deep voice. "I KILL THE MOCKINGBIRD!"

Michael glances around at the chaos Elena's made. "This is like Disney meets dystopia," he says.

Elena ignores him and points at the walls around us. "We'll make copies of that ransom note they showed on TV. We'll tape them to the walls so that people will get the point."

Mort looks around at the mess. "And what exactly is the point?"

"To get people's attention," explains Elena.

I stare at the bloody hatchet, and the Christmas lights and the ruined books that are piled up around Santa. I can only imagine what it looks like from the sidewalk. "This will definitely get people's attention."

"I'm not sure if that will be a good thing," says Mort.

"Listen," Elena tells her uncle, "right now, everybody is talking about I Kill the Mockingbird. You said so yourself. With this display, it won't be long before they'll be talking about you."

Mort gives a little laugh. "You're right about that."

"So what do you think?" she asks.

Michael just shakes his head. I can't take my eyes off the blade that Santa Claus is plunging into the pages of my favorite novel. "I thought it was a sin to kill a mockingbird," I offer in a tiny voice.

That makes Mort laugh again. "I tell you," he says, "I think the bookselling business gets more exciting every day."

# 16
# The Mockingbird Manifesto

· · · · · · · · · · · · · ·

*Elena, Michael, and I continue our meetings in the* bookshop after the store is closed. We use Mort's computer to post anonymous comments on Twitter. We also share photographs I've taken of hatchet-wielding Santa Claus on Facebook and Instagram. I use my real name when I upload the shots.

"Are you sure that's a good idea?" Michael asks me.

"People know that the three of us work here," I tell him. "If we post the pictures anonymously it will look like we're trying to keep a secret."

"We are trying to keep a secret," Michael reminds me.

Elena covers her face with both hands. "A veil of truth conceals a web of lies," she announces.

"Who said that?" Michael asks.

Elena uncovers one eye. "I did. Just now."

"And anyway," I say, "we want people to know where Kris Kringle the Book Murderer is located."

"Why?" asks Michael.

"We promised Mort that we'd get him some publicity."

Not surprisingly, the Internet decides that Santa with an ax is a topic worth trending. It doesn't hurt that a couple people almost as famous as Wil Wheaton mention us online, too.

"Who's Chuck Wendig?" Elena asks one evening.

"You're kidding," says Michael.

"What about Cory Doctorow?"

Michael's head shoots up. "No way."

"Neil Gaiman?"

"You guys," says Michael, "this is getting out of control."

Pretty soon, Santa Kills the Mockingbird is not just the buzz of the Internet, it's also the talk of the town. People drop by to take their own pictures of the display window, and soon, Mort is selling *To Kill a Mockingbird* faster than he can keep books in stock. "It's still strange that nobody has stolen a single one of my copies," he says on an afternoon when it's just Elena and me in the store.

Elena flips through a bunch of old vinyl singles that Mort sells out of a wooden crate. "West Glover is not a high crime area," she says without looking up.

"And the shop is very small," I add. "It would be difficult for anybody to get away with it."

"We could leave the store unlocked at night," Elena suggests.

"Let's not," says Mort just before he heads upstairs to get some lunch.

As soon as the door closes behind him, Elena and I rush to the computer. Bookstores around the country are reporting I Kill the Mockingbird activity now. It's become almost impossible to find copies of the novel in New England or in any of the mid-Atlantic states. Several stores in Colorado, California, Oregon, and Georgia say they're missing books, too.

"This is insane," I say.

"This is awesome," says Elena.

In the meantime, we've posted a statement on our web page to hopefully control people who might think that stealing the books is a good idea. We call it THE I KILL THE MOCKINGBIRD MANIFESTO. It says:

WE SUPPORT ALL ACTIONS THAT LEAD TO THE JOY, THE FUN, THE REWARD, THE CHALLENGE, AND THE ADVENTURE OF READING. WE DO NOT CONDONE THIEVERY, VANDALISM, OR CRIMINAL BEHAVIOR. WE ENCOURAGE THE USE OF RESOURCES SUCH AS WIT, COURAGE, HUMOR, AND FORBIDDEN FRUITS. TRICKERY, DISRUPTION, CIVIL DISOBEDIENCE, MILD CHAOS, AND COMMUNITY ACTION . . . THESE ARE PERMITTED, TOO. WE FIGHT FOR THE BOOKS!

Elena added the last sentence. She wanted to add a sort of *Braveheart* feel. To me, it sounds more like *The Lorax*, but that's not a bad thing.

"We know people are talking about the book," I say to Elena. "I wish we could be sure that they're reading it."

"How about we go online and start a rumor that *To Kill a Mockingbird* is violent and lewd?" she suggests. "That would get people to read it."

"The story's got rape, murder, lynching, and rabies," I remind her. "There's also a man named Boo, an old lady drug addict, and a kid dressed up like a pork chop. How are we going to top that?"

Elena shrugs. She grabs a handful of records from the wooden crate and stacks them onto the record player. She hits a switch, and one by one the records drop onto the turntable while we sweep and dust the store. Mort returns from lunch just as a new song begins. The tune opens with a couple sharp drum beats then rolls into something with a flute and a jangly guitar.

"What is this?" Mort hollers over the music which is turned up way too loud.

I'm standing near the turntable so I glance at the record. "Sugarcubes," I shout.

"Is that the song or the name of the band?"

"I have no idea!"

"Don't worry," Elena calls before her uncle can respond. "Ignorance has not held us back yet."

Over the next few weeks, we continue visiting local stores and libraries. We hide books whenever we can, but it's becoming more and more difficult. At several locations, there are signs explaining that *To Kill a Mockingbird* is now kept behind the counter and is only available upon request. At Millrace Books, a tiny store in Farmington, the owner has the novels stacked inside a fancy brass birdcage secured with an antique padlock at the center of her store. "That's good," Elena says when we find the display. But the three of us still like Santa better.

The next day, Dad corners me in the kitchen. I made some hummus for lunch, but Mom doesn't want to eat it. "Lucy," Dad says when he sees me, "we've got to talk."

Mom is in the backyard taking photographs, so Dad and I are alone in the kitchen.

"About what?"

"Stephanie Buskirk is coming to visit me in my office tomorrow."

"Michael's mom?"

Dad nods. "Officer Buskirk."

"What does she want?"

Dad looks toward the back door. It's clear that he's checking to be sure we won't be interrupted.

"Mom is outside taking pictures of bugs," I tell him. "She didn't eat any lunch."

"She'll eat when she's hungry."

"I don't think she's getting enough sleep," I say.

"She'll sleep when she's tired."

"Have the doctors—?"

"Lucy," Dad interrupts me. "I'm trying to tell you something."

"What?"

He leans toward me and speaks in a low voice. "I think there's a detective on your trail."

I don't reply.

Dad grabs a spoon, scoops some of my hummus onto a tortilla chip, and takes a bite. "I've been spending some time on I Kill the Mockingbird dot com."

"Oh?"

"Nice photographs." He takes another chip. This time, he digs right into the bowl. "And I like the I Kill the Mockingbird Manifesto, too."

"That's good."

"So what should I tell Officer Buskirk?"

"Tell her I said hello."

"You know what I mean."

"Hello!" Mom calls from the doorway.

Dad jumps back and so do I. "There's still hummus!" I blurt out.

Mom makes a face and heads toward the refrigerator. "Do we have any ice cream?"

"You should be eating healthy foods," I tell her.

She turns to face me. She looks annoyed. "Are you free this afternoon?"

"For what?"

"Simple photo shoot," she says, "but I could use an assistant."

"Sure."

"You don't have other plans?"

Michael is playing baseball all day, Elena is working at the store, and Mort doesn't need me. "Nope."

"Good," says Mom. "Meet me at the car in ten minutes." She grabs a handful of chocolates from a wooden bowl and leaves the kitchen.

"You didn't answer my question," Dad says in a low voice.

"No answer is an answer," I tell him.

"Is that what I should give Officer Buskirk?"

"That works for me."

# 17
# What I Want

. . . . . . . . . . . . . .

*A half hour later, Mom and I are standing in the cemetery* across the street from St. Thomas United Church of Christ. The church, all worn red brick, is located in the far west end of West Glover. Mom parks the car beneath a big weeping willow, and then we wander among the battered grave markers.

"What are we doing here?" I ask.

"Location shots." Mom kneels down, balances her camera atop one of the headstones, and points the lens at the bell tower above the church's double-door entrance. When there's time, she likes to drive around and take pictures of local churches in all kinds of different light and weather. That way, she always has extra photos to add to couples' wedding albums. But this church hasn't seen a wedding—or any other kind of service—for a long, long time. The windows are boarded up. The doors are chained shut, and the front steps are covered in dirty brown leaves that look like they've been here for years.

I point at the building. "You need pictures of this?"

"Not really."

"But you asked me for help."

"I lied."

"Then why are we here?"

Mom lowers her camera. "There's something I want to tell you."

"What is it?"

"Lucy," says Mom, "here's the thing . . ."

I feel my heart begin to speed up. "Is something wrong?"

"I don't like hummus."

"Excuse me?"

"Hummus," says Mom. "It's like garlic peanut butter except it's made out of beans."

"Okay," I say.

Mom continues. "I don't actually like salads or soups or lentils, either. Also, I wish you'd stop trying to get me to eat so much fresh fruit. It gives me a stomachache."

My mother has just listed most of the foods that I've been trying to put in front of her since she got home from the hospital. "But—"

"And there's one more thing."

"What?"

"Lucy," says Mom, "I am going to die."

Suddenly I feel like I can't catch my breath. "What?" I say again.

"You heard me."

A cicada's whine splits the air. A pair of swallows darts past my head. "You brought me into a cemetery to tell me this?"

Mom reaches out and squeezes my hand. "It seemed appropriate. But that's not all."

"There's more?"

"I am not going to die today."

I pull my hand away from her. "What are you talking about?"

"Of course I could get hit by a school bus or accidentally electrocute myself or something, but that's unlikely. It really would take some kind of weird, long-shot mishap for me to be dead by tomorrow or even the next day."

"Are you going to die or not?" I ask my mother.

Mom points at the gravesites all around us. "We all die, Lucy. Me. You. Everybody. But you know what we do first?"

I shake my head.

"We pretend that it's not going to happen. We make believe that we're never going to die. Do you know what that's called?"

"Lying?" I say.

"Living, Lucy. It's called living. That's what I'm going to do now. So please stop tip-toeing around the house because you're afraid that loud noises might disturb me. Please stop giving me carrots and granola and organic skim milk. Please stop looking at me like I might fall and break into a million pieces any minute. It's depressing."

"Milk is good for your teeth!"

"I had cancer," says Mom, "not cavities."

"What do you want to eat?"

"A hot dog would be nice."

"Hot dogs? Why don't we just go buy a bag of chemicals so that you can gobble it up with a spoon?"

111

"We did that," says Mom. "It was called chemotherapy. It saved my life. Now I'm going to eat what I want."

"What exactly are you trying to tell me?" I say.

Mom stares at me for a moment before answering. "Be happy."

"Be happy?"

"Be happy," she says again.

"That's it?"

Mom shrugs. "That's all I've got."

I lean against a nearby grave marker. Mom swings her camera up and before I can protest, she snaps a couple of pictures of me. "Can you please stop?" I say.

She lowers the camera.

"I mean can I say something?" I ask.

"Of course you can," Mom tells me.

"Would it be so hard for you take a little better care of yourself?"

"I take care of myself."

"You don't!" I yell at her. "You eat junk. You don't sleep. No wonder you got cancer!"

"Lucy," Mom says, "you don't catch cancer."

"You don't seem to be trying to avoid it either."

"That's not fair," says Mom. "Do you think I wanted to get sick?"

"Of course not, but—"

"But what?"

"You were dead!" I holler. "The doctors told us that you were going to die. You don't remember, but we were in your hospital room, and we kissed you goodbye." I start to cry. "And now you're alive. It's like a miracle. It should mean something. It's like a second chance. When something like this happens to people, they change their lives."

"You want me to change my life by eating more fruit?" Mom says.

"I don't know what I want." But then I think about what Michael said about me, and I realize that I do know what I want. I just have to say it. "Mom," I begin. "I love you. And Dad loves you." Now I'm sobbing as if my mother really did die. "And I want you to take care of yourself as if you really believed it."

"Oh, Lucy," says Mom.

A gentle wind moves through the cemetery and rustles the trees so that a soft *shhhh, shhhh, shhhh* fills the air around us.

"I'm sorry," I say. "You were so sick. I was so scared." I'm just blubbering now, but I can't stop. "I'm still scared."

Mom opens her arms and I rush into them. "It's okay to be scared," she whispers to me. "I'm scared, too. But we can get through this."

"How?" I ask.

"Together, Lucy. We get through this together."

# 18
# The Secret Circus

· · · · · · · · · · · · ·

*Michael lifts a cardboard box filled with used books onto* Mort's counter, and I start sorting through them. People are always leaving cartons and grocery bags filled with worn titles at the shop's door. I guess they feel bad about throwing books away. Mort asked Michael and me to see if this week's contributions include anything worthwhile, but I can already see that most of it is going to end up in the recycling bin.

"My mother is asking Mockingbird questions," Michael whispers to me.

"I know," I say.

Elena ran out to get us some lunch. Mort is assembling a new set of bookshelves along the store's back wall. There are Christmas carols on the record player again, and a bluesy, big-voiced soul-singer is belting out *I Saw Mommy Kissing Santa Claus*. For some reason, the way the singer draws out the word *I* . . . makes me think of St. Lucy with her eyeballs on a plate, and, God forgive me, I laugh out loud.

"What's so funny?" Michael asks.

"The song," I tell him.

Just then, Elena enters the shop with our lunch. "What's going on?"

"Lucy thinks that kissing is funny," Michael tells her.

I toss an old Scrooge McDuck comic book at him. "I do not."

"It is kind of funny if you think about it," says Elena. "Who decided that smashing faces together would be a good way to improve a conversation?"

"You think it's a conversation?" Michael asks.

"It is if you're doing it right," Mort hollers from the back of the store.

"Remember when Mr. Nowak told us that being a good reader is like having a good conversation?" says Elena. "I bet good readers make good kissers."

"That's not what I was laughing about," I tell my friends.

Elena places a bag of sandwiches on the counter then heads toward the stairs. "I'll be right back. In the meantime, maybe the two of you want to have—" She makes air quotes. "—a conversation."

She leaves the two of us alone at the counter. Suddenly, we both find the pile of used books incredibly interesting. Around us, tiny specks of dust sparkle in the summer sunshine that's pouring through the bookshop windows. Meanwhile, the Ronettes or the Crystals or the Bobby Soxers are still singing about Santa.

The lunch bag between us reminds me of Mr. Nowak who said I should enjoy every sandwich and be brave and pay attention to the world and share beautiful things.

Somehow, those thoughts lead me to Mom who wants me to be happy and eat more hot dogs. And then there's Michael who believes that I am brave and that I should say what I want. And he's right.

"So . . ." Michael finally says.

Before he can continue, I lean forward and just barely brush Michael's lips with my own.

"Hey!" Mort yells at us. "That's enough of that!"

I feel my face turn beet red. "We were just—"

"I don't want to hear it," says Mort. "You've got work to do."

I push a strand of hair out of my face. I feel a little bit breathless. I don't even know if what just happened counts as a real kiss. If it was, it was the tiniest kiss in the history of the world. On the other hand, it felt pretty big to me.

A moment later, Elena returns with napkins and water bottles and chips. "What did I miss?" she asks.

I feel my face begin to burn again. "Uh . . ." I say.

"Ummm . . ." offers Michael.

Elena nods. "You kissed him, didn't you?" she says to me.

"I—"

Elena holds up her hand. "Stop," she says. "Don't talk."

"But—"

"I'm serious," she says. "If you talk, you're going to ruin the moment."

I open my mouth, but before I can speak Elena pops a chip into it. Suddenly, my tongue is on fire, my eyes are watering, and I feel like I'm going to gag.

"Smoky jalapeño bacon," Elena says to me. "Do you like it?"

I shake my head. "No!"

She holds the bag toward Michael. He pushes it away. "I'm good."

I take several huge swigs out of my water bottle. "You're not just saying that?" I finally ask him.

"I'm not saying anything," he replies.

My heart is pounding. I'm not sure if it's from the kiss, the conversation, or the snack food. "Why not?"

"I'm trying to not ruin the moment."

I grab a napkin and try to wipe the taste of pork rind, hot pepper, and house fire off my tongue.

Elena rolls her eyes. "It might be too late for that."

Michael smiles. "It's not."

We eat the rest of our lunch mostly in silence. When we're done, I glance at the clock and realize that a transit bus will be heading to the mall in just a few minutes. Somehow, this seems like a better idea than hanging out shoulder to shoulder inside Mort's shop for the rest of the afternoon. "Anybody want to visit Mr. Dobby?" I ask.

"If you're going, we're going," Elena says. "We're the three musketeers."

"Or the three stooges," offers Michael.

"Or the three little pigs," I say.

Elena crumbles up the sandwich wrappings and tosses the balled-up paper at me. "Who are you calling little?"

A few minutes later, we step inside the mall. I wish I was holding Michael's hand, but we'll be heading in different directions once we get inside. Over the summer, we've learned that a teenager shopping alone gets almost no attention—and no assistance—from your average retailer. On the other hand, three teenagers shopping together make some people want to call in a SWAT team.

Once we get to Mr. Dobby's bookstore, I wander into the children's section. *To Kill a Mockingbird* copies are shelved there sometimes, but today I find nothing but titles and characters that are like old friends to me. There's *Because of Winn Dixie, Officer Buckle and Gloria, Ella Enchanted,* Harry Potter, *The Tiger Rising,* the Grinch, Emma Jean Lazarus, *Pictures of Hollis Woods, Lizzie Bright and the Buckminster Boy, Shark Wars* . . . Elena and Michael tease me about my love for *Shark Wars,* but I don't care what they think. Talking sharks are cool, and not every book has to be a classic.

In the meantime, I'm still sort of shocked at what I did back at Mort's. I kissed Michael Buskirk. At least I think I did. I wonder if he thinks that I did. If Elena is right, Michael and I have started a conversation. But haven't we kind of been having a conversation for our whole lives? That's what friends do. But this is something new.

I take a picture book off a shelf and stare at the cover. Its title is *The Secret Circus.* I laugh out loud. This whole summer has been a secret circus. On the book's cover, a group of tiny, smiling mice peer over the edge of a hot-air balloon basket as they soar over nighttime Paris. Behind them, the city and the sky and even the brightly lit Eiffel Tower are simply drawn. I don't see a circus anywhere. I'm guessing that the story inside this book is not really about the circus at all. I bet it's about all the ways that those mice love each other and care for each other and even make each other crazy. That's my favorite kind of story. It strikes me that I'm living that story—secret circus and all—right now.

A familiar voice interrupts my thoughts. "Hello there!"

I turn and see Mr. Dobby heading toward me. "Oh," I say. "Hello."

Behind Mr. Dobby, Elena pokes her head out from the other side of a tall bookshelf. Just across the aisle from her, Michael does the same thing. The expressions on their faces are part terror and part—okay, it's all terror.

"Hello," I say again to Mr. Dobby.

"I remember you!" he says. "You're the young lady that crashed into Romance."

"True Crime," I tell him.

"No," he says. "It was definitely Romance. What are you doing here?"

"Umm . . ." I wave *The Secret Circus* at him. ". . . shopping?"

"Alone?"

"I . . . uh . . . Why do you ask?"

He glances around as if somebody might be spying on us. Michael and Elena duck behind cardboard displays. "Have you heard about the Mockingbird conspiracy?"

I stare at him blankly. "Are you talking about *To Kill a Mockingbird*?"

He nods. "That's right. The whole thing has me keeping a very close eye on school-age shoppers this summer. I'm sure that a good girl like you is not involved, but—"

"What whole thing?"

Mr. Dobby steps back. His eyes open wide. "You don't know?"

"Know about what?" I ask innocently. At the same time,

I look over the store manager's shoulder and catch a glimpse of Elena and Michael quickly stuffing books behind nearby shelves. I'm not sure whether to laugh out loud or run for my life.

Mr. Dobby lowers his voice. "There is a secret and ongoing plot to prevent people from reading *To Kill a Mockingbird*!"

"There is?" I say.

He taps a finger on the picture book in my hand. "Never mind *The Secret Circus*. This is a conspiracy!"

"*To Kill a Mockingbird* is on my school's summer reading list," I say.

"Do you have a copy?" Mr. Dobby asks me.

I nod. "It's my favorite book."

"You are very lucky."

"Why do you say that?"

"Not everybody has been able to get their hands on the novel," he explains.

Behind Mr. Dobby, Michael and Elena finish their shelving and head for the exit. "Do you have copies available?" I ask the store manager.

"I do," he says proudly. "A shipment arrived earlier today. It's the first time we've been able to carry the book in weeks."

"I know that some of my friends haven't read it yet," I say. "Do you think I could get a copy for them today?"

"You can!" exclaims Mr. Dobby. "Just follow me!" He leads me past history and electronics and rock 'n' roll. I see shelves filled with philosophy and baking and war and ballet. There's even a display dedicated to zombie and vampire defense. I hope I never need one of those books, but I'm glad they're here in case I do. In fact, I'm glad that all the books are here. The whole store reminds me just how much I love to read.

In front of me, the store manager comes to a very sudden stop. "Mr. Dobby?" I say. "Is everything all right?"

Mr. Dobby says nothing.

"Are you okay?" I ask.

Mr. Dobby points at an empty shelf in front of us. "They're gone."

"What do you mean?"

"Gone!" The little man is on the verge of tears. "They're all gone!"

"*To Kill a Mockingbird?*"

He nods.

"Maybe somebody bought them," I suggest.

Mr. Dobby shakes his head. He reaches out and pulls down the paper flyer that's taped to the wall behind the empty shelf. He hands the little poster to me. I read the page aloud.

"I Kill the Mockingbird."

# 19
# The Second Most Exciting Funeral of All Time

· · · · · · · · · · · · · ·

*"That was a close one,"* Michael says once we step aboard the bus heading back to West Glover.

Elena points at the bag I'm holding. "It couldn't have been that close. Lucy had time to shop."

I take a seat as the bus lurches forward. "You weren't standing next to Mr. Dobby when he started to cry. I had to buy something." I pull *The Secret Circus* out of my bag. "Also, I really wanted this book."

Elena plops down beside me. Michael sits in the row ahead of us. He turns to face Elena. "Where did you hide your Mockingbirds?" he asks.

"Ornithology," she replies.

"You hid *To Kill a Mockingbird* with the bird books?" I ask.

Elena shrugs. "I was being ironic."

Michael pulls out his phone and punches at the screen. "I put mine behind True Crime."

"We are not criminals," I say.

"Not true criminals." Elena leans into me as the bus swings out of the mall parking lot.

I point at Michael's phone. "Who are you calling?"

"I'm not calling anybody. I keep a list on my phone of all the places we've hidden books in case we ever get a chance to put them back."

Elena shakes her head. "All the king's horses and all the king's men—"

"—probably wouldn't be enough to put all these books back where they belong," Michael says.

They're both right. Books are going missing all over the country now. I can't imagine how we'll ever be able to put them all back. This morning, we found online newspaper reports of I Kill the Mockingbird activity in Montgomery, Alabama; Salt Lake City, Utah; Madison, Wisconsin; and Spunky Puddle, Ohio. "If we've made it there, we've made it everywhere," Elena said when we saw the news from Spunky Puddle.

Michael's reaction was a little different. "This is seriously out of control."

Neither Elena nor I could disagree. On the bright side, every one of those articles mentioned a surge of renewed local interest in To Kill a Mockingbird. In Madison, the disappearing books inspired a local theater group to stage To Kill a Mockingbird in a public park. In Montgomery, the local library announced plans to host a day-long, community-wide To Kill a Mockingbird read-aloud. Anybody can stop in, step up to the podium, and recite a few pages. There are rumors that Harper Lee herself might be there, if not in person, then in spirit. In Spunky Puddle, the mayor invited all one hundred seventy-two Spunky Puddle citizens to join him for the movie version of *To Kill a Mockingbird*, which he'll be showing on the back of his barn on Saturday night.

But then I think about Mr. Dobby. The look on his face was devastating. He was totally crushed when he found the empty shelf covered in I Kill the Mockingbird flyers. Not only that, even though we don't want to admit it—not to the world and not to ourselves—there are people out there who are stealing books under the I Kill the Mockingbird flag. We started this whole thing to do something good, but now bad things are happening, too. "You know it's time to end this," I say to Michael and Elena.

Michael looks up from his phone. Elena turns in her seat to face me. "Lucy," she says, "we can't just shut it off."

"We have to," I tell her.

"But it's not just the books. It's all the people who joined us online too."

I look at Michael. "How many do you think there are?"

He shrugs. "Dozens. Hundreds. Thousands . . . Who knows?"

Outside, cars and trees and people glide by our windows. They are unaware that the fat, blue bus rolling past them contains a trio of radicals, rebels, and literary terrorists.

"We have to end it," I say.

"What if we can't?" asks Elena.

"We can," I promise.

The bus goes over a big bump as if the road beneath us disagrees.

Elena sighs. "But how?"

"We'll just have to figure it out," I say.

"We'll need a big finish," she tells me.

"We'll need to not get caught," says Michael.

"That would be good, too," Elena agrees.

The bus takes a sharp corner then comes to a stop beside the Federal Green. It's late afternoon, the sky is blue, and the air smells like freshly cut grass. We're the only ones getting off in West Glover, so we thank the driver then head over to the bleachers at the baseball field. A couple of T-ball teams are playing something that looks like baseball. I see Michael's mom kneeling next to a little girl who is wearing a batting helmet the size of a spaghetti pot. Officer Buskirk, still in her police uniform, whispers into the girl's ear, and then the two of them break into laughter. A moment later, the child steps into the batter's box. With her tongue sticking out the side of her mouth, she stares at the ball, which is resting on a black tee in front of home plate. Suddenly, the girl swings clean and fast. The ball leaps off the end of her bat and flies far and deep into center field.

"What did your mom say to that girl?" I ask Michael.

He shrugs. "She says something different to everybody."

"Is it always the right thing?" Elena asks.

He gives a little smile. "Pretty much."

We cheer for the little girl as she sprints around the bases. By the time she tags third, we are jumping up and down and screaming out loud. Michael's mom sees us and starts to laugh. "SAFE!" we all shout when the girl slides into home.

Officer Buskirk gives us a big smile and two thumbs up. "Your mom is proud of you," I say to Michael.

He nods.

"Is that why you're so good?" Elena asks him.

"I'm better than I'd be without her."

"Is that why you don't want to get in trouble?"

"Probably," he admits.

A loud *PING!* from another aluminum bat connecting with a baseball interrupts our conversation. The three of us turn to watch several small fielders run around with no apparent destination. Finally, the ball turns up in one of their gloves. From there, the game quickly turns into a mix of catch and tag and brawl. "I'm beginning to understand why they call this America's pastime," I say to Michael.

Elena shakes her head. "It's like you can't look away."

"It's because you don't want it to end," Michael tells her.

"You know," Elena says after a moment, "I really don't want to go to high school."

"High school will be fine," I promise.

"That's easy for you to say. You're tall and smart, and now you've got a boyfriend."

"Right," I say. "Everybody in high school wants to be friends with geeky girls shaped like skyscrapers. As far as having a boyfriend, we hardly kissed."

"But you will."

I shift uncomfortably on the hard bleacher seat. "We'll see," I say.

"Hello," says Michael. "I'm sitting right here."

"I just mean that it's too soon to call you my boyfriend," I explain.

"Fine," says Michael, but he sounds annoyed.

"I wouldn't mind calling you my boyfriend one day," I tell him.

"Really?" he asks.

"Really."

Elena rolls her eyes. "Well that didn't take long."

"Elena," I say, "you're pretty, you're smart, and you're funny. High school boys are going to fall all over you."

"That's because they'll trip on me before they notice I'm there."

"You'll cut them down to size," I say.

"And then you'll have them where you want them," Michael tells her.

That makes Elena laugh.

"If you want them at all," I add.

Elena sighs. "You really think it's going to be all right?"

"I know it will." I remember what Mom told me back at the cemetery. "Because we're going to do it together."

The three of us sit quietly for a while. We watch the tiny T-ball players skip and run and laugh as they chase a bucket of tennis balls that Officer Buskirk has tossed onto the infield. Suddenly, Elena blurts out a question. "What if we throw a party?"

"For what?" says Michael.

"That's how we can end the whole Mockingbird thing."

"A funeral for the Mockingbird?" I ask.

Michael looks up at the sky. "We weren't supposed to kill it."

"We didn't," says Elena. "And it won't be just a funeral. It will be more like a festival."

"That's not a bad idea," I say. "Remember what Father Wrigley told us at Mr. Nowak's funeral. It wasn't just an ending."

"It sure wasn't," says Elena.

"How are we going to throw a funeral?" Michael asks.

"We'll send out invitations," says Elena as if it's obvious. "And we'll post it online, too. People from school and around town can come. Maybe our friends on the Internet will come, too. Even if they can't, we'll let them know that it's time to put everything back where it belongs." She looks around the Green. "We can do it right here!"

Michael looks at Elena as if she's lost her mind. "What happened to not getting caught?"

That stops Elena, but only for a second. "We'll just have to do it in secret."

"Are you serious?"

Elena stands and points at the park around us. "There's picnic tables. There's plenty of parking. There's a playground. There's a bandstand. This will work!"

"She's serious," I say to Michael.

"First we kill the mockingbird," says Elena, "and then we throw the most exciting funeral of all time. What do you think?"

I think back to the day we buried Fat Bob. "Elena," I say, "the second most exciting funeral of all time will be just fine."

# 20
# Put Back Your Books or Boo Radley Will Get You

. . . . . . . . . . . . . . .

*We decide that it will all come to an end at the Federal* Green on the final Saturday in August. "That's less than two weeks away," Michael says.

"And then summer's over, and then school starts, and then we're in high school, and then we're grownups, and then we die," says Elena.

"I think what she means," I say, "is that we're running out of time."

We begin by posting messages online, which is tricky because we know that Michael's mom, my dad, and apparently a large part of the world is keeping a close eye on I Kill the Mockingbird now. Our website has been overwhelmed by comments and questions and notes from all over the universe. Some of them are encouraging, some are scary, and some are just weird.

it is NOT a sin to #killthemockingbird

## #ikillthemockingbird MUST DIE

If that **#ikillthemockingbird** doesn't
sing, I'm going to buy you a diamond ring.

"What is that supposed to mean?" asks Michael during one of our late night meetings at the bookshop.

"I think somebody wants to marry us," Elena tells him.

"I'm starting to hate the World Wide Web," I say while we respond to several dozen new Twitter messages and Facebook notes.

"Is it the ability to communicate easily, directly, and cheaply that you hate?" asks Michael. "Or is it the way that the Internet enables a free and unfettered worldwide exchange of information and ideas that brings you down?"

While we're talking, Michael uploads a photo of one of the paper signs we've been posting on phone poles and shop windows and community bulletin boards around West Glover. We sneak around after midnight and slip them beneath windshield wipers of parked cars, too. The signs feature the same cryptic message with a bird at the center of the bull's-eye. But this time, the bird is dead.

Weirdly, it seems like there are a lot more signs around town than just the ones that we've been putting up. "People are helping us," says Elena.

"Who?" I ask.

She shrugs. "This has taken on a life of its own."

Actually, that's not totally true. We've discovered several good strategies for giving ourselves more life than we really deserve. First, we communicate every day with anybody and

**i KiLL thE MOCKiNGbiRd**

**FINAL SATURDAY IN AUGUST**
**SUNDOWN**
**WEST GLOVER FEDERAL GREEN**
**www.iKILLtheMOCKINGBIRD.com**

everybody who stops by one of the Mockingbird sites. We also send notes to folks who haven't visited in a while. Second, we spend as much time as possible on various online book discussion groups where we comment often and include links back to our own pages. Finally, we start flame wars with ourselves. Basically, we use fake accounts to say really stupid things on our Twitter feeds and Facebook comments. Because so many smart people are our friends and followers now, dozens of them immediately jump in to correct misinformation and come to our defense. Getting a really good flame war started can bring in a hundred new fans. Our biggest success occurred when Elena suggested that *Forrest Gump* was actually a sequel to the movie version of *To Kill a Mockingbird*. Nearly a thousand angry people joined that conversation. More than half of them stayed with us when the shouting was done.

In any case, slowly but surely, a new kind of I Kill the Mockingbird message is starting to spread.

> **#ikillthemockingbird** RETURN POLICY =
> YES.
>
> PUT BACK UR BOOKS OR BOO RADLEY WILL
> GET U **#ikillthemockingbird**
>
> HOW R **#ikillthemockingbird** BOOKS LIKE
> SWALLOWS, BOOMERANGS, ZOMBIES, AND
> JESUS? THEY COME BACK.

Online, we post a link to the Mockingbird Manifesto at least once a day.

> WE SUPPORT ALL ACTIONS THAT LEAD TO THE
> JOY, THE FUN, THE REWARD, THE CHALLENGE,
> AND THE ADVENTURE OF READING. WE DO NOT
> CONDONE THIEVERY, VANDALISM, OR CRIMINAL
> BEHAVIOR . . . WE FIGHT FOR THE BOOKS!

I'm not sure that it will be enough.

In the meantime, we're starting to hear a general buzz and questions around town. Several strangers start to drop by Mort's bookshop. They are mostly young and smart and friendly. They come into the store to buy books, and they take photos of our novel-killing Santa with their cell phones.

"Do you know anything about the Mockingbirdpalooza?" a college-age boy asks me the day before the party. He's wearing plaid shorts, plastic sandals, and a brown concert T-shirt from some band called The Loom. A big, black gym bag is slung over his shoulder.

I glance at Elena who is pushing a broom near the shop's front door. "Mockingbirdpalooza?" I ask.

"We think your town is sort of the epicenter." The boy is cute, but not as cute as Michael, who has a baseball game today. "A bunch of us drove in from Providence to see what it's all about."

Mort looks up from his computer. "Whatever it is, it's been great for business."

A tall Asian girl joins the boy at the counter. She's wearing a long, baggy blouse over a halter top and black leggings that stop at her knees.

"Soo thinks it's some kind of locavore movement for books," the boy explains.

"Loco-what?" asks Mort.

"Are you part of the event?" she asks.

"We think there's going to be a free concert or something," says the boy.

Mort eyes the college kids. "Why would there be a concert?"

"To focus attention on so-called great books," says the girl. "But not all of them are necessarily that great."

"I Kill the Mockingbird is about killing off a few classics and making room for new ones," says the boy.

Elena turns to face him. "I don't think that's what it's about."

"Whatever it is," he replies, "it got us to read the novel again."

"Really?" I say.

"Definitely."

"Did you like it?" I ask him.

"I totally lost it when Atticus shot that dog."

"Me too!"

"Then you've got to come to Mockingbirdpalooza." The boy turns to Mort. "And bring Santa too!"

"I don't do paloozas," Mort says.

"Check this out." The boy unzips his bag. First he pulls out a ukulele. Next he finds a small tablet computer. He stuffs the ukulele back into the bag then places the tablet onto the counter. We all gather around him as he uses his computer to pull up our website. Michael has added lots of bells and whistles to the website since summer began. As soon as the page loads, a big, bold drum-driven tune begins to play while a message scrolls across the screen.

JOIN A POWERFUL WEST GLOVER GATHERING TO KILL THE MOCKINGBIRD.

"I love this song," says the girl.

"Hmmm," says Mort.

The boy clicks over to our Instagram page where a dozen

different photos show Santa Claus in Mort's window. "Who took these?" asks Mort.

The boy shrugs. "Lots of people. Your Santa is a total online celebrity."

In addition to Mort's shop, there are also several pictures showing I Kill the Mockingbird bookstore displays that have popped up around the country. A few of them feature their own Santa Claus dolls.

"Interesting," says Mort.

In the comments sections of the pages, people are debating the merits of various novels. They're yelling at each other and suggesting alternate summer reading plans. There are also bunches of links to articles and essays and book reviews. In addition to all that, it looks like a lot of folks are planning to visit West Glover soon. Mort points at the little computer. "This looks like part Woodstock and part military invasion."

"And part dumb luck," I mutter.

Elena jabs an elbow into my ribs.

"What?" says Mort.

"Nothing!" we say.

But for just a moment, I consider confessing everything. There's a part of me that wants the whole thing to be over. And part of me simply wants to brag. I'm glad that all our work has convinced people—even if it's just two college kids from Providence—to read *To Kill a Mockingbird*.

"Promise you'll be there," the boy says.

"It will be fun," says the girl.

Mort considers the college kids. "What are your names anyway?"

"I'm David Donovan," says the boy. He points at his friend. "This is Callie Soo Bendickson."

The girl holds her hand out to Mort. "My friends call me Soo Bee."

Mort shakes her hand. "When is this palooza thing happening, Soo Bee?"

"Tomorrow night."

"On Federal Green," I add.

Everybody turns toward me. Elena gives me a dirty look. I feel my face burn red. "That's what the signs say."

"Do you want to go?" Mort asks Elena.

She shrugs. "Soo Bee says it will be fun."

"Soo Bee Soo Bee Soo," says Mort. "Okay, we'll be there."

"Santa Claus, too?" asks David.

Mort laughs. "Sure. Santa will be there."

"Excellent!" says David. "It wouldn't be a palooza without Santa."

# 21
# Kindling Words

. . . . . . . . . . . . . .

**I'm sitting at the end of the Federal Green bleachers on** the morning of the big party. Or the funeral. Or the palooza. Or whatever we're calling it now.

Down on the field, Michael is playing baseball. The air above the outfield has that wavy look that happens when too much heat gets mixed with too much humidity. Even the bench beneath me is warm. I didn't tell Michael or anybody that I was coming to the game. I don't even know what inning it is or who's winning. I don't really care. I just like watching Michael play.

At the plate, a batter takes a sharp cut and fires a line drive. The ball ricochets off the pitcher's glove which turns it into a high, spinning pop fly. Michael, who is playing second base, turns away from the pitcher and breaks into a sprint toward the outfield. "I GOT IT!" he yells. Without looking back, he sticks his glove up. The ball lands in his palm with a solid *smack!*

"He's not bad," says somebody nearby.

I turn and find my mother standing beside me. She's got a camera around her neck and another one dangling over her shoulder. She's also carrying a fat, black equipment bag and several lenses in holsters around her waist.

"Did *Sports Illustrated* send you?" I ask.

She grins. "Something like that."

I nod at all her gear. "Do you need a hand?"

"I'm good," she says.

"You look good," I tell her. And it's true. She really does. She is tan and healthy and strong, and suddenly I want to cry because I'm so happy to see my old mom again. Of course, I'm not going to utter the words *old mom* out loud.

She leans forward and kisses me on the cheek. "I've got to run. I have plans to shoot soccer, basketball, softball, volleyball, skateboarding, tennis, and lacrosse today. If I'm lucky, I'll find a horseback rider, some boaters, badminton, and some stuff I haven't thought of yet, too. I already got a fisherman, a cyclist, a jogger, and now baseball."

"What are you doing?" I ask her.

"Some editor thought it would be a good idea to photograph a whole day's worth of sports in one small town."

"That is a good idea," I say.

She nods and smiles. "Especially since I got the assignment."

"Good luck!"

As Mom heads away, I realize that even though West Glover is not a very big place, there's an enormous amount of activity going on around me pretty much all the time. There are Little League games, literary terrorists, crazy families, cancer patients . . . and that's just at my house. The thought makes me laugh out loud.

"What's so funny?"

I look up and find Michael beside me. The game must be over. Before I can speak, my phone buzzes. It's a text from Elena.

"This place is crazy," I say to Michael.

"You're just now figuring that out?"

I glance down at my phone.

I HAVE AN IDEA, says Elena's message.

WHAT KIND OF IDEA? I type back.

A WONDERFUL, AWFUL, GRINCHY IDEA.

AND? I ask.

MEET ME AT BOOKSHOP. BRING THE TRIKE.

"We're off," I say to Michael.

A few minutes later, he and I roll to a stop in front of the store. Michael is on the tricycle, and I'm peddling my faithful, pink three-speed. Elena meets us on the sidewalk. "We're going to the library," she announces.

"The West Glover Library?" says Michael.

Elena nods.

Michael reaches into his pocket and pulls out his phone. He scans the screen, lowers his voice, and tells us, "*To Kill a Mockingbird* is hidden behind the taxidermy section there."

"Taxidermy?" I say.

"We're not going inside," Elena tells us.

"Taxidermy?" I say again.

Elena ignores me. "We're going behind the building." She

139

steps into the tricycle's storage basket. "I'll ride back here for now."

Michael turns around in the tricycle seat. "This isn't *Driving Miss Daisy*."

Elena laughs. "Just go," she tells him.

It doesn't take long to get to the library. It's only a few blocks east on Main Street. Before we reach the entrance, however, Elena has us turn down a narrow alley. It leads to a small parking lot where we find a squat green dumpster beside a row of bright yellow recycling bins. They're all lined up against the library's back wall. In the heat, the dumpster smell hits us like a fist in the face.

"What kind of library garbage smells like that?" Michael asks.

"Really bad books?" I suggest.

Despite the smell, Elena leads us to the recycling bins. They are all filled with old paperbacks and hardcovers. Many of the books have ripped pages and spines busted open, but a lot of them look fine.

"What are these doing here?" says Michael.

"Libraries have to get rid of old books to make room for new stuff," Elena explains. "It's called weeding. Mort and I used to sift through here sometimes, but volunteers go through it now. They sell anything worthwhile. The funds help the library. The rest gets tossed."

I pull an old brown book from one of the bins. "They're just throwing these away?"

Elena taps a yellow container with her toe. "It's recycling."

I flip through the pages. "This is a perfectly good book."

Michael takes the book from me and reads the title. *"The Travels and Extraordinary Adventure of Bob the Squirrel."* He looks up. "People like squirrels."

"I bet nobody's read that book in years," says Elena.

"So?"

"So if nobody's going to read it," says Elena, "then having *Bob the Squirrel* in the library is like having a rose bush in a vegetable garden. Do you know what that's called?"

"What?" asks Michael.

"A weed. It's pretty to look at, but it won't help you make a salad. Luckily, we're not going to make a salad."

"What are we going to make?" I ask.

Elena starts pulling books from one of the recycling bins. "A bonfire."

"Excuse me?" I say.

"Actually," says Elena as she starts moving books toward the tricycle, "it will be more like a funeral pyre, but instead of a body we've got books."

"I am not going to burn books," says Michael.

"Not just any books," Elena says. "We're going to burn a thousand pages of *To Kill a Mockingbird*."

Michael's mouth drops open as if somebody just punched him in the stomach.

"It's going to be great!" Elena promises.

"Are you out of your mind?" he finally asks.

Elena laughs. "Don't worry. We're not really going to burn *To Kill a Mockingbird*. We're just going to burn pages from these throwaways, but nobody will know the difference once they're on fire."

"You seriously want to set books on fire?" Michael says.

Elena dumps several hardcovers and paperbacks into the tricycle's cargo bin.

Michael crosses his arms. "This is not good."

"It's fine," says Elena. "It won't even be that big of a fire, but it will definitely be a big finish."

Michael shakes his head. "It really is true what they say about the teenage brain."

"What are you talking about?" I ask.

"I read about it in a *National Geographic* magazine," he says. "Our brains go through a massive reorganization starting when we turn twelve. We start losing impulse control. We take big risks. We overestimate rewards. We basically go insane." He points at Elena. "And there's the living proof."

Elena gives Michael a big grin.

"Lucy," Michael says to me, "tell her that you are not going to go along with this."

"It would be a big finish," I tell him. "And we've come this far."

"We're already throwing a funeral!" Michael protests.

"Anybody can do that," says Elena. "But it takes real nerve to host a book burning. Plus," she adds, "if we burn books, we'll get tons of publicity."

"So?" says Michael.

"So more people will hear about I Kill the Mockingbird."

"Enough people have already heard about it."

Elena tosses several more titles onto the tricycle. "But this will get more visitors to the website. We can post your list showing all the places where books are hidden. Libraries and bookstores will get the word that nothing was ever really stolen. Everybody will be able to find everything without us having to go back to the places ourselves."

I turn to Michael. "That actually makes sense."

Michael stares at the library recycling bins for a long time. "What about the books that have been stolen?" he finally says.

"That's not our fault," Elena says.

"It's a little bit our fault," I tell her.

"More than a little," says Michael.

"We can't visit every town in the country to put a stop to this thing," says Elena. "But we can send a signal that it's really and truly over. The bonfire will be that signal."

I turn to Michael. "Do you have a better idea?"

"No," he admits. He turns toward the recycling bins. "Are they really just throwing all these books away?"

"Don't think of them as books," says Elena. "Think of them as kindling words."

Michael sighs. "Can I keep *Bob the Squirrel* for myself?"

I put a hand on his shoulder. "I've already put it aside for you."

# 22
# "It Was a Pleasure to Burn"

. . . . . . . . . . . . . . .

*We bring the tricycle back to my house, roll it into the* garage, and close the door behind us. Mom's car is no longer parked in here, so the space feels huge. "Now what?" says Michael.

"Do you have a plan?" I ask Elena.

"Yes," she tells me. "My plan is to gather a bunch of books and then set them on fire."

"That's not a plan!"

"I didn't have time to work out all the details!"

Luckily, with the end of summer in sight, my father is working long hours to get ready for the new school year, and Mom is out capturing the secret life of athletes in West Glover. We have the house to ourselves.

"Okay," I say, "here's what we do." I grab a big metal trash can and drag it to the middle of the floor. I open the lid, and I'm happy to find that it's empty.

"I cannot wait for this to be over," says Michael.

Elena gives him a sweet smile. "It's not over till the mockingbird burns."

I point to the old books still loaded on the tricycle. "Start ripping pages out then stuff them into the garbage can."

Michael shakes his head. "First you want me to burn them. Now you want me to trash and mutilate them. What happened to 'We fight for the books'?"

"Michael," I say, "we are fighting for the books. Now just start ripping."

Still, I know how he feels. These are real books that we're tearing apart. They hold stories and knowledge and truths about the world. I glance at a few titles that have spilled onto the garage floor. I see *Knitting with Dog Hair, Fancy Coffins to Make Yourself,* and something called *Across Europe by Kangaroo.* On the other hand, a bonfire might not be the wrong ending for some of these.

"Lucy," Michael says to me. "When will your parents be home?"

"I don't know for sure," I tell him, "so the sooner we're done here the better."

We tear the books apart as fast as we can, but it's already late afternoon by the time we're finished. We're barely able to fit all the pages into the trash can. "It's just kindling," Michael says over and over. "It's just kindling."

"It is now," says Elena.

It takes all three of us to load the trash can onto the trike, but we finally get it aboard. We snap on the lid then tie it down with bungee cords. From there, we push the whole thing out of the garage and into the driveway.

"Wait," I say at the last minute. I run back into the garage, grab a book of matches, and stuff them into my pocket. "Now," I tell my friends, "we're ready."

It's a slightly downhill ride from my house to the Green, so Michael is able to pedal the tricycle out of our neighborhood without too much difficulty. He has to go slow, but that makes it easy for Elena and me to keep up on foot. When we finally arrive, the sun is setting over the park. Even in the dimming light, it's easy to see that there's a much bigger crowd here than usual. Most of them are standing around the bandstand. Michael, Elena, and I gather at the opposite end of the Green near the baseball field.

I point at the backstop behind home plate. It's really just a great big chain-link fence. "Let's put the trash can there," I say. "It's surrounded by dirt so nothing else will burn. After the sun goes down, I'll light the pages then find you in the crowd."

"Why are you the one to start the fire?" asks Michael.

"I got us into this," I tell him. "I'm going to end it. Not only that," I add. "I'm the one who brought the matches."

"I want to read something," says Elena. She reaches into her pocket and pulls out a copy of *Fahrenheit 451*, the most famous book-burning story of all time. "This is what gave me the idea for the bonfire."

"That's perfect," I say.

She opens to a dog-eared page and reads aloud. "So few want to be rebels anymore." She looks up. "That's not true for us."

Michael takes the book from Elena, turns to a different

page, and reads. "Let us this day light such a candle that, by God's grace, shall never be put out."

"Good one," I say.

"Okay," says Michael. "Let's do this thing."

Elena rubs her hands together. "It was a pleasure to burn."

That's the very first line in *Fahrenheit 451,* and it makes all three of us laugh, which I am sure is not what Ray Bradbury, the author of the book, ever intended.

Together, we move our heavy container off the tricycle then carry it to the chain-link backstop. Michael takes the bungee cords and uses them to secure the trash can to the fence. "There's no reason it should tip over," he says, "but just in case."

I glance toward the bandstand. The crowd is even larger now, and a group of musicians appears to be setting up instruments on stage. "You two go mingle in the crowd," I tell Michael and Elena. "I'll start the fire as soon as it's dark. I'll join you once I'm sure it's going to stay lit."

"And then," says Elena, "we wander around and tell people that we heard that the bonfire is made with copies of *To Kill a Mockingbird.*"

"Exactly," I say.

Elena smiles. "Excellent."

I turn to Michael. "And are we ready to post the list of hiding spots onto our home page?"

Michael pulls out his phone and swipes at the screen a few times. "As of now," he says, "the I Kill the Mockingbird website features a list describing every hiding spot we know about. Not only that, I made it so that people can add new locations and also make notes on the ones that are already there."

"You're awesome," I say.

"Thanks."

On the other side of the Green, the crowd has drawn close to the bandstand. The sound of music floats across the park. "Is that a ukulele?" I ask.

We stop and listen closely. "Actually," says Elena, "it's a bunch of ukuleles."

"I think they're playing Beach Boys songs," says Michael.

"You should get moving," I tell my friends.

Elena slaps at a mosquito on her arm. "Can I say one more thing?" She doesn't wait for a reply. "I just want to say that I have had a great summer." She points at me. "And so have you." She turns to Michael. "And so have you."

"I can't argue with that," I say.

"Me neither," says Michael.

I watch as my two best friends cross the Green then blend into the crowd. Soon, the stars begin to twinkle in the sky. While my eyes adjust to the darkness, I enjoy this clear, beautiful night that is filled with cricket songs and fireflies and ukuleles. In the distance, I see that the bandstand musicians include the college kids who visited the bookstore earlier today. They have been joined by a banjo player, a few guitarists, and a small girl banging on a bucket. I look more closely and see that the little drummer girl is Ginny, owner of the Norse god wiener dog.

Meanwhile, David Donovan, the boy who spoke to me at the bookshop, has his head bowed down, and he's strumming on his ukulele as if somebody might die if he stops.

I don't recognize the song, but people are clapping and dancing and singing. I don't understand all the words until that girl Soo Bee steps up and wails into this big megaphone-bullhorn thing. "With my lightning bolts a glowing, I can see where I am going . . ." She takes a breath and repeats the line. "With my lightning bolts a glowing, I can see where I am going . . ." She looks so brave and bold up there. The musicians behind her are playing for all they're worth. I think she's going to repeat the line again, but instead she smiles at the crowd and yells into the bullhorn, "You better look out below!"

The song ends with a sudden, unexpected chord that every player hits simultaneously. The musicians must be as surprised as anybody because they all burst out laughing while the crowd, which has grown to several hundred people, explodes into cheers and applause.

This, I realize, is as good a time as any to start a fire. As quietly as possible, I remove the trash can lid and place it in the dirt. Luckily, there is no real wind so I don't have to worry about littering the park with loose pages from *Knitting with Dog Hair*. I pull the matches from my pocket, but then I stop. For a just a second, I think I hear something in the dark. I stand frozen in place. The sound comes again. It could be a bird rustling in a nearby tree or it could be gravel crunching beneath someone's foot. "Is someone there?" I whisper.

"It's me." Elena steps out of the shadows.

"And me." Michael is here, too.

"What are you doing?" I ask.

"We couldn't leave you alone," says Michael.

149

"But—"

"Actually," says Elena, "we can't let you go through with this."

On the bandstand, the musicians begin another song. It's the tune we embedded onto the home page of our website. I shake my head. "But the bonfire is your idea," I say to Elena.

"I know," she says.

"Elena and I were talking," says Michael.

"The more we talked," says Elena, "the more we started to realize that the bonfire is not a good idea."

"I don't understand," I tell them.

Elena points toward the bandstand. "Look. All those people are having a great time. They're making music and talking about books and making new friends. It's exactly what Mr. Nowak was talking about when he told us about being good readers. And we made that, Lucy. If we light this fire, that party is over."

"But what about I Kill the Mockingbird?" I ask. "How can we end it?"

Michael steps forward and takes my hand. "I think you know."

Elena takes my other hand. Together, the three of us cross the Green. From the bandstand, David Donovan and his friend Soo Bee see us coming. They wave us forward until we are on stage with them. "Hey!" says David. "Are you having fun?"

"Do you play an instrument?" Soo Bee asks me.

I shake my head. "I have to tell you something."

"What is it?" she asks.

I spot the megaphone at her feet. "Can I use that?" I ask.

"There's no rule that says you can't."

I pick up the bullhorn and turn toward the Green. I push a button on the handle and assault the crowd with an ear-splitting squeal.

"Not that one!" David yells. He reaches over and points to a switch that activates the megaphone.

"Hello?" I say. My voice echoes across the field. The crowd is surprisingly quiet and attentive. So I begin. "We wanted to do a good thing," I say. "And I think we mostly did."

There's some scattered applause.

"No," I say. "You don't understand. I killed the mockingbird . . ."

Elena leans toward me and speaks into the microphone. "And I killed the mockingbird."

Michael joins us too. "I killed the mockingbird."

"I kill the mockingbird!" somebody shouts from the crowd.

"And I kill the mockingbird!" a second person adds.

"I kill the mockingbird!" several more folks shout out.

"No!" I say. "Stop!"

The crowd goes quiet again.

"Here's what really happened."

And then together, Michael, Elena, and I confess everything.

# 23
# Spanking the Critics

. . . . . . . . . . . . . . .

*The next morning, we're inside a gray, windowless meeting* room at the West Glover police station. I'm perched on a rickety, metal folding chair, which is making my bottom cold. Mom's on a creaky wooden seat to my right. Dad leans on the table in front of us and stares at his hands. Across from me, Michael, Elena, and Mort sit uncomfortably, too.

"How are you doing?" Dad asks quietly.

"I'm okay," I say.

"You don't look okay," says Mom. I notice that her cheeks have color now from spending time in the summer sun. Her hair is wild but not in an angry, unhealthy hospital bed kind of way.

"I'm just tired." I was up for most of the night. After we told our story, the crowd at the Green decided we were heroes. Except for Mort. He decided that we were not. He made his way to the bandstand, shoved Santa Claus into Elena's arms, and ordered us home.

Mom, Dad, and Mrs. Buskirk met us at the bookshop where Mort turned on his computer, and we watched the I Kill the Mockingbird comments roll in. According to the Internet, we were inspired geniuses, selfish pranksters, spoiled brats, leaders of an organized-crime syndicate, and a new type of action-oriented literary critic. The on-line world agreed that we should be sent to jail, offered movie deals, awarded medals, featured on our own reality TV show, and given spankings.

"Everybody always wants to spank the critic," said Elena.

"Everybody might not be wrong," said Mort.

"What were you thinking?" asked Mrs. Buskirk.

"We were thinking about how to get everybody to read *To Kill a Mockingbird*," Michael explained.

I turned to my dad. "We were thinking about Fat Bob."

He raised an eyebrow. "You did this for Mr. Nowak?"

Now, Michael's mother enters the interview room and takes the chair at the head of the table. She places a folder on the tabletop. "Thanks for coming in," she says. "Who is going to explain what's been going on?"

Michael raises his hand. "Can I ask a question?"

"You are not at school," his mother says sternly.

He lowers his arm. "Is anybody under arrest?"

Elena sits up straight. "Nobody should be talking if we're under arrest."

Officer Buskirk shakes her head. "Nobody is under arrest."

"Promise?" says Michael.

His mom nods. "I promise."

"Wait a minute." Elena leans forward. "It is a well-known fact that police officers can lie to suspects."

Officer Buskirk sighs impatiently. "You are not a suspect, and I don't lie."

"You could be lying right now," Elena replies.

Officer Buskirk's eyes narrow.

"Elena," says Michael, "my mother doesn't lie."

Mort puts a hand on Elena's arm. "Let's hear what everybody has to say."

Elena crosses her arms and leans back in her seat.

"Start with the book burning," Officer Buskirk tells us.

A fluorescent bulb in the center of the ceiling flickers on and off as if this is a scene from some old-time TV crime drama.

"There was no book burning," says Michael.

His mother raises an eyebrow.

"We got paper from the recycling bins at the library," Elena explains.

"And we never actually set it on fire," adds Michael.

"Can we get our garbage can back?" Dad asks me.

I realize that the trash can is one of a million loose ends that I didn't think about. "I'll do my best," I promise.

"What about the mob scene at the park?" asks Officer Buskirk.

Mort gives an unexpected laugh.

"What's so funny?" she asks him.

He shakes his head. "I was there. There were ukuleles."

"So?"

"It can't be a mob if it comes with ukuleles."

"Fine," says Officer Buskirk. "Let's talk about the string of robberies that's been taking place at virtually every bookstore in the area."

Mort stops laughing. "Not every bookstore."

"There were no robberies," says Elena.

Michael shifts in his chair.

"Not locally," she adds.

I clear my throat.

Elena sighs. "Not that we're aware of."

Officer Buskirk lifts her manila folder off the table. She opens it, pulls out the poster with our little, dead mockingbird, and waves the sheet of paper at us. "I've got printouts from a dozen different websites and discussion groups all talking about I Kill the Mockingbird this and I Kill the Mockingbird that. But they're not just talking about West Glover. They're talking about activity all over the country. How did you do this?"

Above us, the lightbulb makes a loud snap, crackle, and pop. I shuffle my feet beneath the table. I'm trying to think of a good answer to Officer Buskirk's question, but nothing comes to mind. "You know," Elena finally says, "it really wasn't that hard. It was like opening a jar of lightning bugs. They all just came flying out."

Dad leans forward. "Have any laws been broken?" he asks.

I shake my head.

"No," says Elena.

"We don't think so," says Michael.

Elena turns to Mort. "I'm sorry we didn't steal your books."

Mort sighs. "It's okay."

Officer Buskirk rolls her eyes. "What am I supposed to do with you three?"

"We did confess," I say.

"In public," adds Elena.

Mort laughs. "It's true. The three of them looked like they were going to pee themselves up on that bandstand."

"It was really scary!" protests Elena.

"Good," Mort tells her.

We sit around the table for a long time without speaking. Finally, Michael breaks the silence. "What's going to happen now?" he asks.

Officer Buskirk still has our flyer in her hand. She glances at it one more time then pushes it toward the center of the table. "That's a good question," she says. "It's up to you three to come up with a good answer."

# 24
# Ordinary Time

. . . . . . . . . . . . . .

*Elena stands on the Federal Green bleachers and jumps* up and down. "Let's go, Michael! Let's see what you can do!"

It's the ninth inning, and Michael is at bat. It's the last game of the summer season, and the sun is slipping low in the sky. It's been over a week since Mockingbirdpalooza, and there's no evidence in the park to suggest that anything special has happened here this summer. But I know better.

Down on the field, the pitcher goes into his windup and release. At the plate, Michael watches the ball without taking a cut. "Good eye!" yells my father who is seated behind me.

Mom, Mort, and Mrs. Buskirk are here too. "Lucy," Mom says to me, "guess what I got at the snack stand?"

I turn to look.

"Vanilla ice cream with a strawberry on top," Mom says proudly.

"A real strawberry or a strawberry Peep?"

She laughs. "That sounds kind of good."

Meanwhile, Michael is waiting for the next pitch. A moment later, the ball comes flying toward the plate. "You can kiss that one goodbye," says Dad.

Michael takes a small step forward. He swings his hips around. His arms, shoulders, and bat follow. There is a loud *PING!* and the ball springs off the end of the aluminum bat as if it's loaded with dynamite.

"All right!" shouts Elena.

"They're going to have to send a boat to get that one," says Mort.

"The river is half a mile away," Elena tells her uncle.

"Who said anything about a river?" asks Mort. "Look out Moby Dick!"

"Do not ruin this ball game by talking about literature," says Mrs. Buskirk.

"Sorry," says Mort. "All mentions of the great American novel shall cease and desist."

Michael crosses home plate, and the opposing players begin to yell encouragement at their pitcher.

"We're still up by one!"

"Give 'em the cheese."

"Let's end this thing!"

The street lights around the Green begin flickering to life, which makes a bird in a nearby tree start to complain. *Squack! Cheep! Chirrrrrupp! Tweee-twee-twee. Squack! Cheep! Chirrrrrupp!* The song goes on and on.

"That sounds like a mockingbird," says Mort.

Officer Buskirk throws up her hands. "Did you hear what I was saying to you, old man?"

"I'm serious!" says Mort.

Mom puts a hand on Mrs. Buskirk's arm. "Stephanie," she says. "It *is* a mockingbird."

"You can't arrest him for being right," says Dad.

Mrs. Buskirk gives my father a dirty look.

"Maybe she can," says Mort.

"Do they always have to be this annoying?" Mrs. Buskirk asks Mom.

She nods. "They do."

Over the last few days, Michael, Elena, and I have personally contacted every store and library within a hundred miles. We've apologized to everybody and also put all the books back where they belong. Actually, there were a few we couldn't find so we had to pay for them. We've also reached out to other bookstores and libraries around the country. We offered to pay for any of their missing books, too. We've received some harsh replies, but only a few places have asked for money so far. Finally, we met with Mr. Dobby around a table in his bookstore coffee shop. "What you did was very wrong!" he told us.

"Mr. Dobby," said Elena, "I don't think—"

"What she means to say," said Michael, "is that we are very sorry."

"I do not accept your apology!"

"You don't?" I asked.

"There's no need to apologize! We're selling books like hotcakes! Our corporate office is building next summer's marketing campaign around your concept. We're calling it I Harpoon the Whale dot com. What do you think?"

"I think you should pay us for that," said Elena.

"I think not," said Mr. Dobby.

There are two outs now, a man on base, and honestly, I'm ready for this game to be over. I'm even ready for summer to be done. School starts in a couple days, and I want things to get back to normal. As Dad likes to say, it's time for some ordinary time. In our church calendar, Ordinary Time is when we're supposed to be living our lives without feasting or penance or other drama. It's not a quiet time exactly. It's more like the days are supposed to be filled with expectation. That sounds about the right speed for me at the moment.

Elena turns to face the bleachers behind us. "Mr. Jordan," she says to my father, "do we really have to take English from Miss Caridas again this year?"

Dad keeps his eyes on the game. "Actually, no."

This is news to me. "Oh?"

"She got married over the summer. When she comes back, she'll be Mrs. Peckett."

"But she'll still be the same teacher," I say.

"Not exactly," says Dad. "She heard about everything you did this summer for Mr. Nowak."

"Uh oh," Elena mutters.

"All the teachers have been talking about it," Dad continues. "If you're a teacher, you dream about having students who will try to change the world someday because of something you do or say in the classroom."

Elena grins and nudges me with her elbow. "That's us. We did it."

Dad nods. "Yes," he says. "But do me a favor and don't do it again until you've graduated from college."

"What about Mrs. Peckett?" I ask.

Dad raises an eyebrow. "I have a feeling that class with Mrs. Peckett will be a little different than class with Miss Caridas. I've noticed that she's one of several young teachers carrying planning books inscribed with the initials W.W.F.B.D."

I turn to my father. "Where did those come from?"

"From me," he says simply.

"Thanks," I tell him.

"Say thanks to Fat Bob," he replies.

"Do you think he's listening?"

Dad shrugs. "Saying thank you never hurt anybody."

Just then, the *ping* of the bat interrupts our conversation. It's a long, fly ball to right field. If it clears the split rail fence that divides the ballpark from the rest of the Green, Michael's team will win the game. The opposing team's center fielder sprints away from his pitcher. Runners are racing around the bases and toward home. The fielder reaches the fence and leaps. His foot lands on the top rail. He springs up and executes a pirouette-like spin in midair. He stabs his glove high into the air. Miraculously, the baseball smacks into the leather.

"Wow!" says Dad.

We watch as the boy floats backward then tumbles into the grass. He lies there for a moment then pops up with the ball in his hand. Every person—spectators and players alike—leaps to their feet and cheers.

"That was awesome," says Mort.

"Good catch," says Mrs. Buskirk.

I look down at the dugout and find Michael. He is shaking his head and smiling. Even though the game is over and his team defeated, he hops onto a wobbly bench near the dugout and applauds the player who is jogging back toward the infield with the ball. Michael turns his attention to the stands, catches me staring at him, and waves.

"I'll be right back." Before Mom and Dad can answer, I hop down the bleachers and trot toward the dugout. I find Michael standing near home plate watching me approach. "Good game," I say when I reach him.

"We lost," he points out.

Around us, players from both teams gather up gloves and bats and balls. Most of them smile and laugh when the outfielder who made the magic catch gets wrapped up in a big hug from a woman who must be his mom.

"Of course," says Michael, "if you have to lose, it's not a bad way to go."

"That's how I feel about our summer," I tell him.

He nods. "Except that we didn't lose."

"No," I say. "We really didn't."

Our conversation is interrupted by a couple older boys who approach Michael and give him high fives. "We wish you were on our team next year," they tell him.

Michael just smiles.

"Won't you be playing with them in high school?" I ask when they walk away.

"They're in college," he explains.

"Oh."

Michael reaches out and takes my hand. We start walking toward the bleachers together. "So what happens now?"

I think about what Officer Buskirk said at the police station. "That's up to us," I remind him.

"That works for me," says Michael.

"Me too," I tell him.

I look around the park. I see family and friends everywhere I turn. Mom has an arm around Dad as they work their way down the bleachers. Elena is making Mort and Mrs. Buskirk laugh. The sky above us is turning dark blue, and Michael's hand is warm and strong in my own.

As we walk off the field, a light breeze lifts a scrap of white paper off the ground. It blows against the leg of a nearby baseball player. He picks it up, reads it, and then waves it at his friends. I recognize the bull's-eye and the bird from here.

"Hey!" the kid hollers, "did anybody read that Mockingbird book this summer? It was awesome!"

# ACKNOWLEDGMENTS

· · · · · · · · · · · · · · ·

The very first spark for *I Kill the Mockingbird* began with a conversation about summer reading lists that started on blogs including Pam Coughlan's *Mother Reader*, Colleen Mondor's *Chasing Ray*, Leila Roy's *Bookshelves of Doom*, and Elizabeth Bird's *A Fuse#8 Production* among others. Barely a day goes by that I don't learn something new and also laugh out loud because of these fantastic writers and their peers in the incredible community of kidlit bloggers. I was also inspired by friends and fellow writers who encouraged me to read early pages of the manuscript aloud at the wonderful Kindling Words retreat in Vermont. Thank you to Marnie Brooks, Allison James, Tanya Lee Stone, and all my KW friends. Your overwhelming kindness, enthusiasm, and laughter turned a small spark of an idea into a bit of a bonfire.

My heartfelt thanks go to super friend, co-conspirator, and remarkable editor, Nancy Mercado. Somehow, in a few slap-dash lines and notes, she saw an entire novel. Not only that, she believed that I could write it. Nancy is truly a co-creator in this work. Thanks also to Simon Boughton and the entire team at Roaring Brook and Macmillan for bringing this book to life.

I owe special thanks to my everyday heroes including Michelle Acampora, David Donovan, Scott Hardek, Mark Harris, Joyce Hinnefeld, Greg Lasalle, David Lubar, John and Geri Ann McLaughlin, Kathy Rooney, Ruth Knafo Setton, Melissa Starace, Virginia Wiles, and many others. I don't know what I would do without you. Also, my wife, Debbie, and my children, Nicholas and Gabrielle, deserve a special note: You keep me sane, laugh at my jokes, help me stay focused, and encourage me to keep going. I love you with all my heart.

During the writing of this book, both of my parents went ahead and survived bouts with cancer so that I'd have even more authentic material to work with. Thanks, Mom and Dad. Next time, please limit your assistance to old photos, family stories, encouraging words, and good meals.

Finally, thank you to Harper Lee for *To Kill a Mockingbird*. If you haven't read it, you really should.

# I KILL THE
# MOCKINGBIRD

. . . . . . . . . . . . . .

## bonus materials

# SQUARE FISH

## I KILL THE MOCKINGBIRD
by Paul Acampora

**1.** Lucy, Michael, and Elena have been friends forever, but now their friendship is changing. How? Why?

**2.** Describe the different roles that teachers—including Miss Caridas, "Fat Bob," and even Lucy's Dad—play in *I Kill the Mockingbird*.

**3.** According to the Guinness Book of World Records, the heaviest person on record weighed approximately 1,400 pounds. Why do you think the author describes Fat Bob as weighing 4,000 pounds?

**4.** What are some things that Michael does not like about *To Kill a Mockingbird*?

**5.** "When you want something," says Michael, "it's like admitting that your life has a hole in it." What are some things that Michael, Lucy, and Elena really want? And what holes are they each trying to fill?

**6.** How might the story be different if Michael or Elena or one of the adult characters were telling it?

**7.** Why did Lucy think that the *I Kill the Mockingbird* plot was a good idea? Do you think it was a good idea? Why did her friends go along with it?

**8.** Could the situation presented in *I Kill the Mockingbird* have taken place before the Internet?

**9.** Name some books, movies, or music that you think everybody should know about. Why are these works special to you? Why should they be special to everybody?

**10.** At the end of the story, a big bookstore chain announces plans to mimic the I Kill the Mockingbird conspiracy with a campaign called I HARPOON THE WHALE. What will it take for I HARPOON THE WHALE to make *Moby Dick* irresistible?

# GO FISH

## PAUL ACAMPORA

© Adam Atkinson

**What did you want to be when you grew up?**
I planned to be an astronaut, a veterinarian, a fighter pilot, an engineer, a musician, a farmer, a florist, a travel agent, a truck driver, or a gardener.

**What's your most embarrassing childhood memory?**
When I was five years old, I accidentally cut off my sister's ear. I really did feel bad about it. (But not as bad as my sister!)

**What's your favorite childhood memory?**
I can't pick just one. Here's a few that I still think about: playing the piano with my grandfather . . . building a soapbox derby car with my dad . . . Saturday morning tag sales with my mom . . . summer days on Rhode Island beaches . . . bodysurfing gigantic waves after a storm . . . autumn leaves piled higher than my head . . . riding a pony named Misty in the Mum Festival Parade . . . my sister and I eating ice cream cones at the Naugatuck Valley Mall . . . listening to aunts and uncles tell stories over long, slow meals . . . wandering around the library after school . . . sneaking my dog into my bed . . . sipping a Coke on my grandparents' back porch . . .

I've got lots more where those came from. I am very lucky that way.

## As a young person, who did you look up to most?

When I was young, my grandfathers seemed about as different as two people could be. One was strong and stern and quiet. The other was funny and musical, and he liked to sleep till noon. One grandfather worked in a factory his whole life. The other owned a music shop with his brother. One had a quick smile and a thick Italian accent. The other was a remarkable horseman, a great storyteller, an easy artist, and a heck of a poker player. I wanted to be like both of them. I still do.

## What was your favorite thing about school?

My favorite thing about school was my friends. I don't mean that I didn't like math, science, history, and the rest. I liked all that a lot. I was a pretty good student too, but friends are always the best.

## What was your least favorite thing about school?

The color green. I went to a Catholic school and had to wear a uniform—green pants, white shirt, and a green tie—every single day. It wasn't pretty.

## What were your hobbies as a kid? What are your hobbies now?

As a kid, I enjoyed playing the piano. I collected coins with my grandfather. My father and I rebuilt an old sports car. Today, I enjoy kayaking with my wife and kids. I love going to the movies. I'm learning how to play the ukulele. I still have the coin collection. It's fun to sift through it and imagine where the old dimes and nickels and pennies might have been before they got to me.

## What was your first job, and what was your "worst" job?

I've had a lot of jobs. For my first job, I cut my neighbors' lawns. Then I delivered newspapers for the *Bristol Press* in Bristol, Connecticut. Some of my jobs have required some pretty dirty work—cleaning out elevator shafts, collecting dirty dishes off a cafeteria conveyor belt, scrubbing middle-school toilets, spraying chemicals onto thousands of tiny, plastic parts—but those jobs have rarely been terrible. The worst jobs are the ones that force you to spend time with sour, petty, unkind people. There's not enough money in the world to make those situations worthwhile.

## How did you celebrate publishing your first book?

I have a day job, and I had to go to work on the publication day of my first book. When I got home, my family surprised me with cake and ice cream and a big sign on the front of the house which said FAMOUS AUTHOR LIVES HERE! That was awesome.

## Where do you write your books?

My schedule is pretty hectic. I try to carve regular writing times into my calendar, but it rarely works. As a result, I write on legal pads and computers and scratch paper wherever and whenever I have a few free minutes. That can happen at my desk during a lunch break, at the kitchen table before everybody's awake, in waiting rooms while my kids dance or act or take music lessons. . . . I really write just about anywhere.

## Where did you find your inspiration for *I Kill the Mockingbird*?

*I Kill the Mockingbird* started in a lot of different places. The first seeds were planted during an online debate about assigned summer reading lists. From there, I took inspiration from a wide range of sources, including my own Catholic upbringing and Catholic school adventures (which I loved), my family's experience surviving various cancers, my obsessions with books, saints, and popular music, and perhaps, most importantly, the good fortune and escapades I've enjoyed as a result of having very good friends.

## When did you first read *To Kill a Mockingbird*?

I first read *To Kill a Mockingbird* in eighth grade. I found it among a pile of paperbacks stacked on a rickety wooden bookshelf in the back of our classroom. The book had a bloody, dead bird on its cover, so I thought it was a crime thriller or maybe a horror novel. Crime and horror were not standard fare at St. Joseph Elementary School, so, of course, I snatched it up right away. The novel was much less and much more than I expected. It still is.

## What type of research did you have to do for this book?

*I Kill the Mockingbird* required a surprising amount of research! I did a great deal of reading about the pros and cons of assigned summer reading, and I examined dozens of schools' book lists from around the country. I read and re-read many of the classics and also read a good deal of literary criticism so that I could present books as fairly and accurately as possible. I read a lot about Harper Lee, author of *To Kill a Mockingbird*, and learned that she is not the recluse that the media likes to portray her as. Rather, she's been smart, passionate, interested, opinionated, and very funny for her whole life. I checked up on baseball facts and saint histories and Internet phenomenon ranging from hashtags and Wil Wheaton to cat videos and the Arab Spring. I listened to a ton of music and read a lot of lyrics too, so that the songs you "hear" throughout the book would be right. I figured out ukulele chords for a couple Arcade Fire songs, and I learned how caskets get lowered into graves, how far a teenage all-star might hit a baseball, and how Martin Luther

King, Jr. spent summers picking tobacco in Connecticut. I also learned a whole bunch about vacation bible school, bird songs, retail inventory control, Christmas traditions from around the world, the Connecticut public transportation system (yes, there is one), and lots more too. Not everything made it into the final version of the novel, but it all informed the choices I made about the story.

## What was your favorite scene to write?

Everything with Balder the Weiner Dog was a lot of fun. Choosing the chapter titles made me laugh out loud. I feel pretty good about the book's last lines. But my favorite scene has to be the nativity photo shoot. It was the very first scene I wrote before I even knew what the book was about. It's also the scene that I probably revised the most. As much as I liked it, I just couldn't get it quite right. I almost cut it out completely, but then in the end—with lots of pushing and prodding and encouragement from my editor—it all finally clicked into place.

## Have you ever started a grassroots campaign of your own?

I've been part of several large and small efforts, including simple clothes drives, used book collections, local political campaigns, and community fund-raisers. The goal is always to make change for the better. My favorite recent crusade was my daughter's HAMSTERS MAKE GREAT PETS campaign. In that case, I'm the one that had to be changed for the better. Her effort was successful, so she quickly followed up with a WE NEED ANOTHER DOG campaign. It was also successful.

**Why Hamsters Make Great Pets!**

*To Kill a Mockingbird* is one of the most famous banned books. Apart from this title, do you have any favorite banned books?

Sadly, so many great books have been banned that it's almost impossible to have a list of totally unrestricted favorites. Some of my favorite banned titles, in no particular order, are:

*The Chocolate War* by Robert Cormier

*Of Mice and Men* by John Steinbeck

*Bridge to Terabithia* by Katherine Paterson

The Harry Potter series by J.K. Rowling

*Speak* by Laurie Halse Anderson

*The Great Gatsby* by F. Scott Fitzgerald

*Adventures of Huckleberry Finn* by Mark Twain

*In the Night Kitchen* by Maurice Sendak

*The Catcher in the Rye* by J.D. Salinger

The Lord of the Rings series by J.R.R. Tolkien

Zachary and his dad make a fresh start
in a new town with the help of new friends,
a quirky community, and the power of forgiveness.

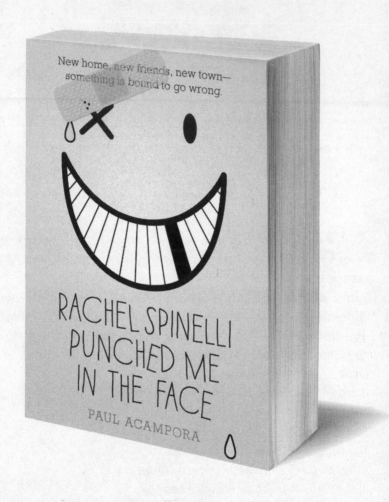

New home, new friends, new town—
something is bound to go wrong.

RACHEL SPINELLI
PUNCHED ME
IN THE FACE

PAUL ACAMPORA

Keep reading for a sneak peek!

# CHAPTER 1

FOR SEVERAL DAYS, AFTER DAD AND I discovered that Mom had gone, we tried very hard to lie. We pretended that she would be coming back even though we both knew better. Dad said things like, "We should paint the kitchen before Mom gets home." I said, "Don't forget to pick up some tea for Mom at the grocery store."

But we couldn't keep it up for long. We never did paint the kitchen. We never did buy the tea. And one night, when Dad put a bowl of spaghetti on the table between us, I said, "Mom wouldn't like this."

Dad took a bite. "Too plain?"

I nodded.

"Your mother's a lot of things," said Dad, "but she's not plain."

Once a week, Mom tried to serve up some kind of complicated recipe made out of strange textures and exotic spices. More than half of those concoctions ended up in the trash.

"You know the difference between my cooking and your mother's?" Dad said.

"Yours tastes good?" I said.

"You got that right."

Dad spoke with a Louisiana drawl he got from growing up in New Orleans. That's where my parents first met. Dad was finishing college and paying for school by playing trumpet with six or eight different bands. Mom was on vacation and noticed my father on the stage of some club. She went to see him play every night until finally he said hello. A few months after that, Dad moved to Copper Lake, Colorado, Mom's hometown. I was born a year later in a spare bedroom at my grandfather's old ranch house.

"Did you and Mom ever think about moving back to New Orleans?" I asked Dad.

"I wouldn't have said no to New Orleans," he told me.

Dad and I ate the rest of the spaghetti without speaking. When we were done, we cleared the table and washed our things in the sink. Finally, I said, "She's not coming back, is she?"

My father hesitated for just a moment before he answered. "No, Zachary. I don't think so." We returned the pot and plates to their shelves, then we stepped outside to watch the setting sun throw strange, brown shadows across the desert. "How about we go for a ride?" asked Dad.

"Okay." I stepped into the passenger side of our old Jeep, and Dad slid behind the wheel.

"Buckle up," Dad told me.

"Don't want to get a ticket, huh?"

"The police around here don't give tickets," said Dad. "They just shoot you."

I rolled my eyes. My father was Copper Lake's lone police officer. "I don't think we'll have to worry about that."

The Jeep started, and we headed west. After a short ride, we pulled onto an old dirt access road and bounced a little farther into rough, open space. Dad shut off the engine, and the two of us stepped outside to sit on the front bumper and stare at the desert. A deep, heavy quiet settled around us. "I never really liked this view," Dad finally said.

"Did you like it when you thought the land might be yours one day?"

Before I was born, my Mom's father owned all the land around us. After he died, my parents discovered that the old man hadn't paid taxes in living memory. Rather than inheriting a thousand Colorado acres, Mom and Dad got a postage-stamp sized lot and the aluminum-sided trailer where we lived.

Dad considered my question. "Honestly," he told me, "I can't say that I did."

At night, Mom used to study maps and memos hoping to find a loophole that would require the government to return the land to our family. "Was there ever really a chance of getting it back?" I asked.

"Nope," said Dad.

I can't say I was disappointed. On one far corner of the property, an abandoned mine pond held an orangey-brown chemical slick that made rainbow patterns in the sun. I saw a duck land in the pond once. The bird gave a frantic quack, a couple flaps, and then it collapsed dead in the water. I wouldn't want to be responsible for that.

I leaned my head back and watched twinkling stars reveal themselves above us. I wish I could say that I knew all the constellations, but my attempts to memorize them always failed. To me, the stars looked like ten thousand musical notes sprinkled randomly across the sky. In the darkening light, I turned and glanced at my father's face. A tear ran down his cheek. I'd never seen him cry. I didn't know what to say or do, but then I remembered Dad's trumpet in the back seat. I grabbed the horn and pushed it toward my father. "Play something."

He shook his head. "You do it, Zachary."

I could play, but not like Dad. I pressed the trumpet into his hands. "Play," I said again.

Dad took the instrument and examined the valves and the brass bell as if he'd never seen them before. Finally, he lifted the horn to his lips, took a breath, and then started to blow.

Before I was born, my father played for big time recording stars and no name brass bands. Now, in the middle of nowhere, he made a song just for me. It soared high into the sky then deep down like a punch in the gut. It was a mad, lonely tune that sounded like coyotes in the desert and my mother sneaking away before dawn. Dad played and played then finally let the last whisper of music fade like a prayer into the desert.

We were both quiet for a long time. "That was good," I finally said.

Dad returned the trumpet to me. "I think we should get away from here," he said.

I stood. "Do you mean away from this spot or away from Copper Lake?"

"I think I mean both," said Dad.

I wasn't sure I wanted to leave Colorado, but staying didn't feel like a solution to anything either. I'd lived in Copper Lake for my whole life, but I didn't feel especially connected to the place. With school a bumpy, forty-five minute bus ride away, my group of friends was small and not particularly close. I'd certainly never had anything even vaguely resembling a girlfriend. And living in a metal box at the edge of town did not put us in the mix of whatever social life even existed in this tiny corner of the world. Now that Mom was gone, leaving felt as sensible as staying.

A few days later, my father told me about a town

in Connecticut that needed a police officer. "What do you think?" he asked.

I sat at our kitchen table. The walls around me were covered with posters that Mom left behind. They were pictures and paintings of faraway places and cruise ship destinations. Months earlier, she'd announced that it had always been her dream to work on a cruise ship. Now I held a short letter that contained Mom's cell phone number, her new e-mail address, and a short note explaining that she'd decided to get away and follow that dream.

"I think that it's not fair that Mom might be in Cancún or Bermuda or Fiji, and we're still checking our shoes for bark scorpions in the morning."

Dad nodded.

"What do you want?" I asked my father.

"I want us to be happy," he told me.

"That's all?"

"That would be enough."

I glanced around our kitchen, which looked like the break room in a travel agent's office. I recalled the arguments, some quiet and some not, between my parents during the past year. There'd been weeks when no more than a couple words passed between them and days when the orange poison pond had been a more pleasant spot than any place inside our house. I turned to my father. "Happy would be nice," I said. "Let's try it."